THIS WILL DO…

Also by Thomas Ogden

Fiction

The Parts Left Out: A Novel

The Hands of Gravity and Chance: A Novel

Non-Fiction

Projective Identification and Psychotherapeutic Technique

The Matrix of the Mind: Object Relations and the Psychoanalytic Dialogue

The Primitive Edge of Experience

Subjects of Analysis

Reverie and Interpretation: Sensing Something Human

Conversations at the Frontier of Dreaming

This Art of Psychoanalysis: Dreaming Undreamt Dreams and Interrupted Cries

Rediscovering Psychoanalysis: Thinking and Dreaming, Learning and Forgetting

On Not Being Able to Dream: Selected Essays, 1994–2005 (available only in Hebrew)

Creative Readings: Essays on Seminal Analytic Works

The Analyst's Ear and the Critic's Eye: Rethinking Psychoanalysis and Literature (co-authored with Benjamin Ogden)

Reclaiming Unlived Life: Experiences in Psychoanalysis

THIS WILL DO…
A Novel

Thomas H. Ogden

SPHINX

First published in 2021 by
Sphinx Books
London

British Library Cataloguing in Publication Data

A C.I.P. for this book is available from the British Library

ISBN-13: 978-1-91257-369-1

Typeset by Medlar Publishing Solutions Pvt Ltd, India
Printed in Great Britain

www.aeonbooks.co.uk/sphinx

In memory of Tom Richardson
(1942–2020)
That morning you died a bird sang
the lonesomest song I've ever heard.

PART 1

BOBBY AND GEORGE

It's a Friday afternoon, after school, early May, and all's right with the world—a feeling never to be had in pure form after you're nine or ten years old. You may think you're having this feeling when you're older, but it simply isn't the same. On just such a day, Bobby Renfro followed a couple of steps behind his older brother George, watching him with the sort of adoration usually reserved for baseball stars. George picked up a stone and tossed it at a tree, and then leaned down to ruffle the soft folds of skin on the back of the neck of the neighbor's dog who was always waiting for them under a shade tree a hundred yards from the foot of their driveway. On reaching the house, George led the way to the kitchen door at the back, and with a grin that lit up the whole house threw the door open with panache.

Once inside, George let his book bag fall with a thud in the corner next to the door and then let his olive-green jacket slide off his back and float through the air before spreading itself lightly over the book bag. Catching Bobby off guard, George turned, stooped, slipped his hands under Bobby's armpits, and with a deep grunting noise, lifted him about a foot and a half off the ground so that their noses were only a few inches apart, and said, "God you're ugly!" and they both laughed a laugh that Bobby had been waiting for all day.

George, a broad-shouldered ten-year-old with blond tousled hair, was hungry all the time. Bobby thought his brother was more handsome than anyone he'd ever seen, even in movies and on TV. His face was just right, his body was just right, everything about him was just right.

George, with Bobby close behind as if carried by George's tail wind, strode across the kitchen to the refrigerator. George opened the fridge, reached inside without using his eyes to guide his hand, and pulled out, as if from the innards of a beast, the can of Hershey's chocolate syrup with its beautiful brown color and not quite shiny silver lettering across its face. There were two dark triangular holes punched on opposite sides of the flat metal lid.

Stepping back a stride or two from the refrigerator, George, with the drama of a carnival sword swallower, tilted his head back as far as it would go, took the can in his right hand, fully extended his right arm, raised the can above his head while slowly tilting the can forward, and poured a continuous thin thread of chocolate syrup into his open mouth onto his tongue, and, when after a full ten seconds he'd finally poured enough, he tilted the can back with such precision that it looked as if he had cut the ribbon of chocolate syrup with a pair of scissors.

He then lowered the can to waist level and ceremoniously handed it to his little brother, saying, "Wanna try it, Bobby my man?"

Bobby gripped the can, which felt much larger and heavier than he'd expected. Stooping down, putting his arm around the back of Bobby's neck, and softly holding his right arm, George said, "Lean your head back over my arm … yeah, like that … and now lift the can slowly … right, like that … and now find the place where your eyes see a tiny bit of the bottom of the can … yes, like that … no, push your arm out straighter … yeah … and now slowly, very slowly, tilt the can forward in your hand … right, like that … and then tilt it just a little more … right … and now open your mouth as wide as you can,

4

and get ready for it to pour, just like that … right … and now very slowly tilt the can until you see the chocolate gather at the front lip … right … and now tilt its front lip down the tiniest bit … a little more … and it will begin to pour … like that … exactly right, just relax and let it make a continuous waterfall onto your tongue, *not* into the back of your mouth or it'll make you choke."

George held Bobby's arm at the elbow more firmly, and supported his neck more sturdily, as a thin thread of syrup began to fall from the can. Bobby, seeming to feel that things weren't lined up right, repositioned himself despite George's efforts to keep his head still. The syrup gathered on Bobby's upper lip and began to move up his face over his cheek toward his right eye. George quickly used his right hand to tilt back the can in Bobby's hand to stop the flow of syrup. "Bobby, you need more practice before you can use the high dive, so for today just pour it into a glass of milk."

"Yeah," Bobby said, sorry to disappoint his brother.

"Don't worry, you'll get it right next time."

George took the dishrag that hung from the handle of the oven, wetted it with water from the sink faucet, and gently washed the chocolate from Bobby's face and shirt, taking particular care in the area of Bobby's eyes.

With all the solemnity of a three-star Michelin chef taking possession of his kitchen, George turned and walked to the bread drawer, untwisted the metal tie at the neck of the white, balloon-covered bag of bread, and gently shook the bag so that a half-dozen slices slid forward in an orderly fashion. George delicately lifted the soft, dazzling white innermost pair of slices from the bunch, placed them on the counter, and then, with a single movement of his hands—like a gunslinger drawing his pistol so fast you couldn't see how he did it—flipped the loaf backward so the slices he had flipped forward took their proper places again, leaving room to reseal the plastic wrapper. With a dinner knife, George confidently spread across the surface of one of the slices a smooth sheet of Skippy peanut butter, only slightly tearing the delicate surface of the airy bread. He then placed the second piece of bread atop the first.

After pouring himself a glass of milk, he carried the plate in one hand, the glass in the other, to his customary seat at the kitchen table, while Bobby took in every detail of this beautiful dance. Slowly, George lifted the sandwich to his open mouth and sunk his teeth into it. He paused between each bite to use his forefinger to remove the peanut butter from the space between his gums and cheek, and then poured the milk from his glass into his mouth, where he briefly held the milk to luxuriate in the taste and sensation before swallowing so hard you could hear the peanut butter-bread-and-milk sludge descend from his mouth, down through his throat, and into his belly.

The two brothers sat quietly after George finished eating. He (George) then pushed the empty plate to the center of the round table, tipped back in his chair, slammed the plastic glass down in front of him, and let loose a belch that came from deep inside of him.

George then prepared a similar dish for Bobby, with the same drama that had marked the preparation and consumption of his own food and drink.

TWO

Bobby and George lived in a world complete unto itself. The two brothers, now eleven and thirteen, were well aware of that fact, but only one of them cared about all that was left out. It was a mid-August day with fall in the wings. The days were shortening, the humidity subsiding, but the heat persisted in their lower Hudson Valley town. Less frequent were the glorious thunderstorms that filled the sky with bright webs that clapped so loud they made believers out of nonbelievers, for despite cool scientific understanding, these bolts could only be thrown at mortal men by gods—or so George liked to say when he and Bobby stood at the windows on the west side of George's room, counting the seconds between the lightning and the slow grumble of thunder.

Bobby sat on the blue-carpeted floor with his legs pulled up, his back to the pale brown wooden cabinet between the two beds. His face and arms were bathed in the warmth of the white sunlight that shone through the leaves and branches of the four maples that stood like sentries outside the four double-hung windows opposite Bobby. It was a large room—the largest of the three bedrooms in the house—with a steeply vaulted ceiling, both sides ribbed by four-inch strips of gray wood, a symmetry that would remain with both boys, not as a memory, but as a part of their sense of their own bodies. Between the gray ribs was textured cardboard-like material that had a slight beige sheen. There were water stains here and there at its lower edges. For Bobby, the stains, like clouds, looked at one moment like human faces only to disappear, replaced by cat-like animals staring down at him, which gave way to the side view of a fleeing bear, and on and on.

Bobby tried not to let his eye focus on a particular water stain at the far end of the room, just to the left of the row of windows. That water stain not only looked like Humpty Dumpty, it *was* Humpty Dumpty, and had been from the time of his nightmare years ago in which Humpty Dumpty looked back at him, laughing, as he began his fall. Despite the fact that he was frightened of Humpty Dumpty, Bobby slept in one of the two beds in George's bedroom because he wanted to be with George more than he was frightened of Humpty Dumpty.

Bobby was content to draw in colored pencils on his pad of thick drawing paper while George worked on one of his model airplanes or warships. The piercing smell of Dope Paint and Duco Cement hung thick in the air. Bobby liked the scent. George sat in a straight-back wooden chair that he pulled up under the shelf that protruded about two feet from the windowed wall and ran the length of the room, some twenty-five feet. Under the shelf were two radiators with space between them where George put his knees and feet—never quite comfortably, it seemed to Bobby.

Though they never spoke of it, they were aware that their parents hardly existed for them, and vice versa. The second floor of the house—where the boys' two bedrooms were separated by a bathroom—stood as a domain in its own right, never having to be defended because no other claims were being made on it. Their parents' bedroom was on the first floor, directly under George's room. Their father had never once, so far as Bobby could remember, set foot on the second floor when he and George were at home; their mother had at one time read them bedtime stories upstairs, but once they no longer wanted that from her, she never climbed the stairs to the second floor when they were in the house, though she left traces in the form of the disappearance of dirty clothes and the appearance of clean clothes and towels in their dressers and bathroom.

Bobby doodled and sketched while he watched George out of the corner of his eye. George pored over instructions printed on a single large, paint-stained white sheet of paper that was machine-folded so many times that it initially fit into a tiny three-by-four-inch packet, but was now spanned out into a two- by three-foot sheet. George, to read it, had to place his eyes a few inches from the tiny black letters, numbers, and diagrams, which looked to Bobby like insects crawling over the page.

George made only American World War II ships—destroyers, battleships, aircraft carriers, submarines—and American fighter planes: Flying Fortresses, Mustangs, Wildcats, and Marauders (which he liked calling by their wartime nickname, "Widowmakers").

Bobby noticed, but never mentioned, that the assembly of ships and planes was far from flawless: painted lines weren't perfectly straight, joints often exuded puckered, half-dried glue, and decals had bubbles of air under them. Bobby also noticed, and never mentioned, that George did not seem knowledgeable about, or even interested in, the story of the war or the role that each of the ships and planes had played in battle. When George told the story of one or another of his model ships and planes, it was clear to Bobby that his brother was making up most, if not all, of what he was saying. George was a docent in his own museum of invented things, with Bobby the only visitor the museum ever had.

When a model was completed, George would step back and look at the collection of model planes and ships that he had arranged at the far right end of the shelf. For a newly completed model, he created a place among the other planes and ships that seemed right to him, a grouping shaped by an aesthetic that was for a long time unfathomable to Bobby, but eventually became discernible. Bobby, with time, began to appreciate the way in which the groupings within groupings of models elicited a feeling in him that each part of the whole conversed with all the other parts. A ship placed just so, several feet from the rest of the fleet, seemed to Bobby to create a shape for the feeling of lonesomeness at the margins, and also the honor that was due to the outcast. Other arrangements of planes and ships were powerfully expressive in shapes that seemed to be continuously moving—an effect created (or so it seemed to Bobby) in the way that the curvilinear line of a battleship's protruding hull led the eye up to a complementary curve at the junction of the wing and fuselage of a transport plane, and then along to other shapes that seemed incomplete on their own. Bobby never spoke with George about these observations because he knew comments of this sort annoyed him.

Sometimes Bobby would take from the waste paper basket a page of directions George had thrown away, which was now crumpled into a ball. Unfolded, it was covered with smears of paint where George had tried out a mixture of tints or wiped his brush, or had squeezed from the tube semi-hardened wads of glue that rose to sharp translucent points, or had discarded torn decals. Bobby, on one occasion, recovered a page of instructions from the floor near the basket, unfolded it, and spread it with the care of a philatelist using tweezers to place a valuable stamp on the table in front of him to examine through a magnifying glass. Having folded it again, he used sharp scissors to cut triangular holes in the dense mass. He asked George to hold it up in front of one of the windows so he could see the effect created by sunlight shimmering through the ragged, quasi-symmetrical field of diamond-shaped holes. George did not return the piece of paper to Bobby and instead placed it on the floor in a corner of the room where neither of them would accidentally step on it.

Sometimes Bobby felt like George's adoring little brother or maybe even his son. But at other times, he felt like George's

10

big brother or his father, because lately George seemed to have forgotten what you have to do if you don't want to look like a freak once you walk out of the front door of the house. George tried to distract both Bobby and himself from this fact by theatrics, such as poor impersonations of real or imaginary people, which embarrassed Bobby.

Bobby, despite his adoration of his older brother, could see that while George was tall for his age, he was so thin he appeared sickly. His arms looked like brittle sticks extending from the sleeves of his T-shirt; his pale complexion and large freckles gave him the appearance of a figure in a wax museum. Bobby, from a distance, had seen George bullied at school. He had been stunned the first time he saw the older boys descending on George, calling him a freak and a faggot. George ignored them at first, but they refused to relent until they succeeded in provoking fear in his eyes—or, best of all, signs of tears.

That summer, toward the end of August, George began to create imaginary battles for his model planes and ships. He would race around the room, a model plane or ship in each hand, making a buzzing sound by vibrating his lips, which created a semblance—a very good one, Bobby thought—of the buzzing sounds of planes in dogfights, the drone of downward spirals, the rat-a-tat-tat of airplane machine gun fire, the swish of the launching of torpedoes, the high-pitched scream of jet engines pushed to their limits as they race down the deck of an aircraft carrier.

When not sputtering and rat-a-tat-tat-ing, George narrated these scenes in the voice of the old newsreel announcers, proudly reporting the successes of "our boys" in Europe and the Pacific. When George tried to speak like Churchill, it became so corny that they began to laugh deep belly laughs and couldn't stop. When one tried to stop laughing, the other would manage to utter one sound effect or another, which would draw them both back into another round of belly laughing. Tears rolled down their faces.

11

THREE

It was late Saturday afternoon in mid-September—Bobby in eighth grade, George in tenth. George missed as many days of school as he had attended this year. The leaves of the maples at the windows of George's room had burst into reds and oranges, which for many would have been beautiful, but for Bobby and George, the fall colors were nothing more than a sign that summer had ended and they were being carried forward by the momentum of time into the Hudson Valley's nearly six-month period of cold, damp air and somber skies. The leaves on the ground outside their windows were pale shades of brown, virtually colorless and as wrinkled as the skin of their grandmother's face. They could almost smell the rotting, worm-eaten, bird-pecked fruit that had dropped from the apple tree just beyond the maples, a tree that never yielded more than small, twisted apples too sour to eat.

The day that would remain emblazoned in the memory of both boys began as an ordinary Saturday at the beginning of the school year. On waking, they could hear the drumming of high-pressure water against metal, and they pictured their father in his khaki Bermuda shorts, no shirt, carefully placing the spray gun handle on the ground and lifting the oversized caramel-colored sponge from the bucket of cold foamy water and swirling the suds over the door or window of their new

Ford Fairlane station wagon with imitation wood paneling on its sides.

The boys hoped he couldn't sense their presence in the kitchen because, if he could, he would yell to them to come out and help. George put the cereal box, bowls, and spoons on the table while Bobby took from the fridge the half-gallon milk carton and placed it on the table. The usual quiet prevailed as the boys read the sports section of *The New York Times* that their father had left neatly folded on the counter under the radio, which was screwed into the bottom of the cabinet above. This was the golden era of the Brooklyn Dodgers: Jackie Robinson at third, Duke Snider in center, Roy Campanella behind the plate. The Dodgers lineup felt to Bobby like the only good sure thing in the universe.

After breakfast, the boys put their spoons and bowls in the sink and retreated to George's room. Bobby sprawled out on the floor with a large pad of drawing paper, along with pastels and charcoal pencils. On the first page of the drawing pad, which he had carefully packed away at the end of the previous weekend, was a half-completed drawing of the back of George's body as he leaned over the ledge where he was working on one of his gray plastic models.

As a gift to his mother, who he knew was feeling sad about something, Bobby asked her to come with him to the toy and hobby store in town where they sold a surprisingly wide array of high-quality pastel chalk, wax crayons, pencils, and thick drawing paper. His mother seemed lost in thought as he moved slowly, deliberately, from one glass case to another. She seemed surprised by the fact that he knew exactly which thickness and size of paper he wanted and which type of crayons and pencils he was looking for. It was not for lack of interest that she didn't ask him what he had in mind to draw or who at school was teaching him to draw; it was by unspoken agreement that she was not to ask him anything about his artwork. And most important of all, she was not to ask him to show her what he drew until he felt he wanted to show her, which she knew he would eventually do because he knew it would cheer her up a little to see them. He was that kind of boy.

That afternoon, Bobby and George had been working quietly for two or three hours when George pushed back his chair and reached under the long ledge below the window sills, trying to find something he'd stored on top of the brown metal radiators. Bobby, lying on his stomach, lifted himself to his knees to try to get a better look. That something unusual was about to happen was no longer a surprise to Bobby. George had for some time now been acting in a way that worried Bobby. He would talk non-stop in bed after they'd turned the lights off to go to sleep, and would continue even after Bobby had fallen asleep (the sound of George's excited exclamations would sometimes wake Bobby).

One of George's favorite things to think about was the mystery of how animals think and communicate. "There's a scientist," George said one night after the lights were out, "a really good one, who said that lots of other animals can think almost as well as humans can, not just dolphins and maybe some birds, like owls, and most of all, dogs, who know what you're thinking and can have a real conversation with you if you pay close attention to the kinds of barking and other sounds they make, and especially the look in their eyes and on their face, and the way they're using their tongue and wagging their tail, and that someday we might be able to have a real conversation with a dog where they'll tell us about what they're thinking, because they think with their sense of smell the way we think with words, and there's a whole way of thinking and feeling and seeing that we don't know about, it's like a whole other dimension, just like you'd never know what sight is if you were born without eyes, you couldn't imagine images, no one could tell you because images just don't exist for a person without eyes, so we don't know what kind of world animals live in because we've been born without a sense of smell that is anywhere as good as theirs and which they use as a language to express ideas in a way entirely different from what we can imagine. Our brains just aren't made that way, so we may never know."

Having found what he was searching for under the ledge, George pulled out a box of wooden kitchen matches. In his mother's hand, the blue and green Diamond Matchbox looked to Bobby like a familiar part of the kitchen that carried an air of danger. In George's hand, it seemed like a loaded gun. The match that George lifted from the box was the usual three-inch wooden one with a white tip and a blue surround—the same type that their mother, with her head pulled back and her arm extended (while Bobby hid behind her, his hands on her hips) held near the hole on the oven floor and waited for the hollow whoosh of the exploding gas, which sometimes reached out of the oven as a faint blue cloud that enveloped the top of her head before making a deep popping sound and disappearing into thin air, leaving behind an odor that was supposed to smell bad, his mother told him, but to Bobby it was the odor he associated with his mother when she wasn't sad, when she was doing something she felt good at.

"Watch this, Bobby," George said in a flat tone of voice, his eyes foggy.

"No, I don't want to watch."

George, now on his feet, took a match from the box and dragged it hard against the rough gray-blue strip on the side of the box until the tip ignited, spitting out tiny fragments of its crust in its always-impressive manner. George turned, and with his free hand reached for one of the planes at the end of his narrow table—one of the smaller, two-engine prop planes with American Air Force decals on the tops and bottoms of both wings and the sides of the vertical tailpiece—a misshapen thing, really, but probably perfect in George's eyes. Bobby could tell that this show was not a game for George; there was no wartime narration this time. It was as if time had stopped; everything was occurring in a still, silent, present moment.

Bobby watched as George held the match flame under the right wing of the plane for a few seconds before the glue caught fire and spread along the seams at the bottom of the plane. They watched the gray plastic become soft, darkening before it spawned a more menacing black-orange flame that transformed the gray plastic into liquid beads that rained down through the air, trailing wisps of black vapor. The beauty, along with the menace of flames and smoke and melting plastic, was not lost to Bobby, but it frightened and saddened him to see his brother in a trance so thick that he seemed no longer aware of Bobby's presence in the room.

As George circled the room silently, holding the burning plane above him, some of the molten plastic dripped into the palm of his hand, but he didn't seem to feel it. The part of the plane that remained intact burned darkly, emitting an acrid odor. The room was emptier now.

As the plane burned, George shifted his hand to the back of it. When the flames that peeked out of the dark black smoke melted the plastic at the junction of the fuselage and one of the wings, the wing flopped into the hollow of George's elbow and clung there still aflame. George made no effort to shake it free or use his other hand to tear it off and throw it to the ground. A moment later, as the remainder of the plane folded into itself, he hurled it through one of the four open windows above his table, the one from which the screen had been removed because the wood frame had rotted.

A sound that was a combination of an embarrassed laugh, a triumphant cheer, and a cry of pain came from George's mouth.

Bobby heard himself saying, "George, I like your planes. Please, don't do that to any of the others."

George lifted from its place in the armada of planes and ships on the far left portion of the ledge one of the larger battleships, about a foot and a half long, equipped with heavy artillery mounted on turrets that encircled each of three tiers above the deck. Tipping it to its side, he held a lit match to the hull just below the waterline where a torpedo would hit it. As the hull caught fire, sheets of flame much larger than those that had come from the plane climbed the side of the hull. George seemed startled by the scale of the fire and the heat it emitted. Large pieces of plastic, parts of which were aflame, fell to the blue carpet, as if falling into the sea.

The burning of the ship was painful for Bobby to watch, but he watched, unable to move or to speak. His paralysis and muteness at this moment remained a source of profound guilt for Bobby for the rest of his life. At times he condemned himself for not having tried to stop George, even though, in another way, he knew he couldn't have stopped him, and he also knew that the thirteen-year-old boy he was at the time loved his older brother more than he loved anyone else in the world. As Bobby watched sheets of burning plastic drop from the deck of the boat onto George's forearm, forming a portion of a molten sleeve, Bobby's heart ached for his brother.

George's eyes were focused on the devastation being done by the flames to the heavy artillery in their turrets and rising up to the bridge, where a tiny figure, presumably the captain, helplessly witnessed the catastrophe before disappearing in the fire.

George seemed not to realize that he had lost control of the situation. Another large glob of burning plastic fell onto his forearm, which made him shake the burnt arm with all his might, causing melted plastic to splatter in every direction, some of which stuck to the right side of his face and neck. He lunged forward, flinging the remainder of the ship out of the same open window through which he'd thrown the remains of the burning plane—though this time, his hurling the ship out the window seemed to be an abject surrender to forces larger than himself. He stood stunned, looking straight ahead, unfocused, through the bank of windows. Absolute stillness enveloped the two boys, stillness devoid of bodily sensation, devoid of thought and feeling, devoid of the movement of time.

Bobby was the first to begin to awaken from this empty daze to find himself in George's room, standing about five feet from his brother, who was standing with his shoulders collapsed into his torso, his arms hanging limply at his sides. His right hand appeared to clasp an object no longer there. Bits of plastic adhered at awkward angles to the right side of his arm and neck and cheek. The expression on George's face was now, for Bobby, the most harrowing part of all of this. On George's face was the expression of death, an expression of all that is not, the face of a body without a person in it.

George—if the body with the expressionless face could still be called George—seemed not to feel the burns to his body. George now seemed to awaken, or maybe just his body did, for he violently ran the back of his left hand from his cheek to the side of his neck, along his arm, and into the palm of his hand, as if a swarm of invisible insects were biting him.

Bobby ran to the bathroom, soaked a bath towel with water, returned to George—who was still swiping at the burns—and pressed the wet part of the towel against the burnt areas, which was difficult to do while George was thrashing about, occasionally landing an inadvertent but forceful blow to Bobby's body.

"Does it hurt a lot?"

"No, not much," George said flatly.

Bobby momentarily stopped patting the burnt areas with the wet towel and forced himself to look closely at George's arm and neck. Bobby was not sure what to make of what he saw. There were purplish, swollen patches that had bits of twisted, black plastic stuck to them, but the skin did not seem to be torn open and the plastic did not seem to be embedded in the skin. Bobby led George to the bathroom where they kneeled next to the tub. Bobby ran cold water from the faucet, turned the handle so only a soft rivulet of water was flowing, and held his brother's arm under the stream.

"Does it feel better with the cold water on it?"

"Yeah … I think so."

After a few minutes, Bobby dabbed George's arm with the dry part of the bath towel. He then walked hesitantly back into George's bedroom, where the air was thick with the odor of smoke and burning plastic. Not knowing why, Bobby began rearranging the model planes and ships on the table by the windows to positions as near as he could remember to the way they'd been arranged before George knocked them around as he grabbed the battleship.

A few minutes after George threw the burning model ship out of the window of his room, flashes of deep orange caught Bobby's eye from the field outside. After momentarily wishing it away as sunlight reflecting off of a piece of glass or metal, his heart sank. The metallic sound of the kitchen screen door slamming ran through Bobby's body like a jolt of electricity. He could tell precisely what was happening. He pictured his father—his Madras shirt hanging over his khaki Bermuda shorts, his tongue protruding from the side of his mouth—running to the toolshed where he kept the fire extinguisher.

When Bobby caught sight of his father coming around the side of the house, he watched him walk quickly—intently—in the direction of the burning field. Bobby went to the window and could see that the fire had consumed some of the grass closest to the house. The next 150 yards of field stretched out to the heavily wooded hills between their house and the ones on the other side. Bobby knew that the distance to the hills was about 150 yards because it was a point of pride for his father when he told people how much open space there was between their house and the one on the other side of the hills.

His father, for as long as Bobby could remember, had been frightened of fire. "This house is made of paper," he'd often say when looking at the cathedral ceiling of the living room of the 1930s craftsman-style house. Now Bobby watched as his father surveyed the situation while standing just outside the border of the burning grass and brush. He shook the rusted metal canister, placed its base on the ground, and repeatedly threw all his weight—which wasn't very much for this thin man—onto the handle of the pump, waiting for the sensation of pressure to build up, but soon seeming to realize that the aged fire extinguisher was worthless. Feeling sorry for his father standing there alone at the edge of the burning field, Bobby raced out of George's room, down the flight of wooden stairs, through the living room, dining room, and kitchen, and out the screen door.

Bobby followed his father back to the toolshed, where he stood timidly at the open door, not knowing what to say. As his father hunted through the row of shovels, rakes, hoes, tree pruners, and rusted saws that were leaning against the far wall, Bobby worried that his father would startle if he suddenly became aware of a presence behind him. As Bobby stood there, his gaze fell on the tool sharpener, a stone wheel about three feet in diameter, at the center of which was a metal axle. You could get the wheel to rotate if you stood behind it and pressed down with your foot on the long wooden pedal. His father had made this by hand.

Bobby thought the tool sharpener was a beautiful thing, but his admiration of his father's abilities as an artisan were vastly overshadowed by his fear of the rage that infused almost everything his father did, particularly when it came to George. His father hated George, as if George had done something terrible, unforgivable, and George hated their father with equal ferocity. Bobby couldn't get an answer from anyone in the family about the origin of his father's anger at George. His father often acted as if George didn't exist—not talking to him for weeks at a time—or screamed at him that he was a disgrace to the family, dumber than dirt, should never have been born, and the like. George would look defiantly into his father's eyes as he cursed George and refused ever to say anything in reply to his father, but made it clear by rolling his eyes that he thought his father was a moron. This hatred between them was the white-hot core of the life of the family, it seemed to Bobby, as he watched his father fumbling through the gardening tools. "Family" seemed to Bobby like a word from a foreign language, a word he could translate but didn't really know what it really meant; he couldn't imagine what it would feel like to be a member of a family in which love and tenderness were the feelings that tied them to one another.

Though his father persisted in giving no indication that he knew Bobby was there, Bobby decided to walk into the shed as if he and his father had agreed that Bobby would help him deal with the fire. Then, taking the largest of the snow shovels, Bobby walked out of the shed, around the house, and up to the edge of the burning field. The fire had spread further than he had expected. A strong breeze had picked up, as it often did in the late afternoon. The substantial trees on the hills posed a far greater danger than the grass and bushes and tangles of blackberry shoots that were now burning.

Bobby's efforts to use the snow shovel to smother the flames quickly proved futile when the junction of the handle and blade bent to a 90-degree angle under the pressure he was putting on it. When his father arrived less than a minute later, carrying a folded canvas tarp, Bobby, without saying a word, helped his father unfold the tarp. Each taking two of the tarp's edges, they carried it to the edge of the fire and lowered it onto a patch of burning grass. Bobby jumped onto the canvas and stamped his feet. He and his father systematically moved the tarp to an adjacent area of burning grass. After moving the tarp three or four times, it became clear that what they were doing was futile.

"Bobby, come with me—I don't want you here by yourself. I'm gonna call the fire department." On his way back to the kitchen, his father saw a slow-moving pesticide tank truck about to pass the foot of the long driveway. His father stopped and waved his arms over his head, yelling, "Hey, Jim! Hey, Jim!" (He always called workers he didn't know "Jim.") The truck pulled into the foot of the drive. Bobby followed his father to the truck. His father stuck his head through the open window of the passenger side of the cab and pointed to the field behind the house, where you could see thin trails of smoke rising thirty or forty feet into the air. Bobby's father pulled his head out of the cab window and told Bobby that the driver said there was still a little pesticide in the tank, and that he'd go empty it out and fill the tank with water.

It was not surprising to Bobby that his father had not called the fire department. His father hated it when other people took over and pushed him aside. What did surprise him was that his father told him what the man in the truck had said.

When the pesticide man returned about a half hour later, he drove the truck a quarter of the way up the incline of the drive-way before turning sharply to the right, moving very slowly, methodically, in order to try to prevent the truck's large wheels from getting stuck in the grass that Bobby's father had planted and took great pride in. As the truck moved across the lawn in low gear, the tires tore deeply into the ground, leaving two parallel trails of dark brown earth bearing the mark of the tires' deep treads.

Bobby was now standing self-consciously next to his father, who was giving hand directions to the driver, even though there was no need to direct him. Bobby and his father watched as the pesticide man drove the truck fifty yards or so along the side of the field, at which point the tires began sinking deeper and deeper into the ground. The pesticide man got out of the truck to have a look at the tires and then walked to where Bobby and his father were standing. He said, "I'm gonna have to drive further from the edge of the fire than I'd like, otherwise the truck's gonna get stuck in the mud. Was there once a swamp here?" His father, impressed, said, "There was a pond, but it was drained before I bought the place. How'd you know?"

"I heard water running in the drain next to the driveway as loud as Niagara Falls, and it hasn't rained here in a couple of weeks. Anyway, let's spray the grass beginning at the foot of the hill and then work our way back to the edge of the fire. The thing we gotta do is drench the grass and leaves at the foot of those hills, where the dry leaves are piled thick at the base of the trees. I'll drive the truck to the foot of the hill and then we'll work backwards toward the house. You spray the grass and leaves beginning at the foot of the hills, and when you've done that, I'll back the truck up and you douse the grass all the way back to where it's burning. It's not a big deal."

Standing next to his father, Bobby noticed that the driver—a short man with a stocky build—was wearing a dark blue work shirt with the name "Boy" stitched in yellow thread just above the left breast pocket. The name made Bobby feel sorry for this man who would always be called Boy.

When Boy had driven the truck as close to the trees as he could get, he left the engine running and got out of the cab. "I get a fair amount of water pressure from the pump in the truck. Don't need it all for spraying pesticide. We'll use most of the water right here next to the hill so the grass'll be wet if any sparks get here. Then I'll back the truck up slowly while you spray till we get to the front edge of where the grass is burning. Stand a few feet from the outer edge and just aim the hose. I'll control the pressure from inside the truck."

Boy then pulled a thick black hose from a compartment on the side of the truck where it was neatly coiled. He screwed a metal nozzle onto one end of it and screwed the other end into a round outlet at the back of the tank. He handed the metal nozzle of the hose to Bobby's father.

As the fire in the low grass and shrubs was doused, thin gray smoke rose lazily from the ground. Working backward toward the house, now midway between the house and hills, the situation seemed to be well under control. The dimming light made the remaining few pockets of flame look like groups of dancers in rich orange cloaks. Then Bobby's father said, "Why don't you do the spraying from here?" in the same tone of voice in which he might ask Bobby to pass the salt at the dinner table. The metal nozzle felt heavier and colder than he'd expected, and the sensation of the power of the water moving from his right hand holding the hose to his left hand holding the nozzle made him feel like Superman. The arc of water onto the flames was graceful, reminding him of the fountains he'd once seen at Rockefeller Center.

When the last of the fire had been extinguished, Bobby could see wisps of smoke floating above the field, a few shades darker than the moonless evening sky. Boy backed the truck across the lawn and onto the driveway and then all the way to the road. Bobby and his father walked the whole distance beside the truck, which felt like the victory lap Bobby had seen the Dodgers take on television after the final out of the final game of the World Series.

Boy climbed down from the truck and stood there quietly with Bobby and his father. His father thanked Boy for turning his truck into a fire truck without a moment's hesitation. Boy put his hand out to shake Bobby's father's hand and then shook Bobby's hand, a small act of kindness and recognition that Bobby would never forget.

"I want to pay you for your time and for the pesticide you emptied from the tank," his father said. "So if you have a pen and paper in the cab, I'll give you my name and address so you can send me the bill." Boy said, "My pesticide costs me something, my time doesn't." He climbed back into the truck and rifled through the glove compartment, which was full of loose papers, spark plugs, and other things Bobby couldn't quite make out. Finally, Boy reached under the driver's seat and pulled out something, which after a few moments Bobby recognized in the dim interior of the cab as a pad with a pen attached to it by a rubber band.

Boy stepped back down from the truck—he was surprisingly agile for a man of his build—and handed it to his father. Bobby was struck by the fact that his father had not told Boy his name, nor had he heard him use Boy's name. They'd worked together for almost three hours without using names. This must be the way men treat one another when they're doing jobs together, Bobby thought: They are generous with their time, they "pitch in"—a phrase his father often used, a phrase his mother would never use—without using names, taking part in something that they, as men, know how to do.

Having neatly folded the hose back into its compartment, Boy slammed shut its metal door. He backed the truck up onto the road. Bobby and his father watched the red tail lights of the truck grow smaller until they disappeared altogether as the truck turned the corner onto the main road.

Bobby and his father walked silently up the stone steps to the front door of the house. Once inside, Bobby turned right to walk through the living room and up the stairs to the second floor, and his father walked in the opposite direction into the kitchen, where Bobby could hear him running the faucet, probably for a glass of water.

FIVE

Bobby's legs felt heavy as he climbed the stairs to the second floor. Once on the landing, he saw that the door to George's room was closed. Bobby knocked softly. He then gently turned the wobbly doorknob and opened the door. He stood at the threshold, where he was met by a warm, almost liquid, acrid stench of urine, burnt plastic, and something else. George had closed all the windows.

Lying on his side on the bed at the far end of the room, George turned his head toward the door. He seemed to have been caught off guard, apparently not having heard Bobby knocking. He rearranged himself into a sitting position on the side of his bed, his stocking feet planted on the carpet.

George appeared mystified as he looked in Bobby's direction. His face seemed featureless, as if there were no bones or muscles in it. Bobby felt a hole in himself in the place George had occupied. Bobby had, for more than a year now, wanted to tell George to try harder, to pull himself together, to return to being the brother he used to be. The two had been gradually switching roles, with Bobby becoming the older brother, trying to protect George from being picked on at school and humiliated by their father. But most of all, Bobby was trying to protect George from knowing what was happening to him. George's stories had become just a flow of words, sometimes making sense but not at all interesting. In the middle of talking about something he had read—such as the fact that we're almost entirely made of air and our solidity is an illusion created by electromagnetic force fields that tie molecules together—George would sometimes suddenly stop, as if he hadn't been telling a story at all. Bobby would try to remind him where he'd left off, but George's attention was by then somewhere else.

It must have been a hard blow to George, Bobby thought, to see and hear him outside with their father. Bobby had been so caught up in the excitement when he saw the flames that he'd put George out of mind. While fighting the fire, he'd thought now and again about how George must be feeling, but had chosen to continue to work with his father and Boy.

Something had gone terribly wrong between George and their father. Bobby didn't understand why his father hated George, and no one would explain it to him. When Bobby asked his mother what had happened to make his father so angry at George, she'd say, "I ask myself that same question." Once she did say more: "I think George reminds your father of his older brother, Harold. He outshined your father—a good student, a good athlete, a good everything. They haven't talked for a very long time, you know." Bobby hadn't known; he knew almost nothing about his father's life. His mother's story was unsatisfying to him, even at thirteen. It didn't explain why his father treated George the way he did.

The room was quiet in a way that was different from anything Bobby could recall. It was now filled with inaudible echoes of the past, the sounds that he and George had made in that room for as long as Bobby could remember—good sounds, the best sounds of his life, the sound of George's voice narrating the basketball games the two of them played with a spongy basketball the size of a grapefruit, and the sounds of his own screams of delight as he'd try to outflank George in his attempt to reach the net, and the hard thumping of George's knees against the floor that shook the whole room as he clomped around the room on his knees to make things even. For another boy, this adoration might have bred feelings of competitiveness, but for Bobby, the good fortune of having George as his older brother was all he could wish for.

George slowly lifted himself from his bed. The stench stung the insides of Bobby's nostrils. Bobby was now certain that George had wet his pants and had lost control of his bowels, but he wasn't sure George knew it. George seemed like a baby whose diaper needed changing. He'd left George alone with the burns. But the burns were the least of it. Far more agonizing, Bobby thought, were George's feelings that Bobby had betrayed him, had left him alone, had chosen their father over him. And on top of that was terrible shame for having started the fire, which proved to everyone in the whole world that he was a pathetic, repulsive, crazy kid who would never come to anything, just as his father had always said. Bobby thought that George must have imagined that he and their father, together with a man George didn't know, were talking about George and laughing at him.

The burns were the least of it, Bobby thought, but still, he had neglected the burns when he tore out of the room to join their father. George needed to be looked after by their mother or father. Their father probably wouldn't want to have anything to do with George. When their father smacked a spoon hard against George's knuckles when George reached for something across the dinner table, George acted as if it didn't hurt—it hadn't even happened.

When Bobby thought of going to their mother for help with George's burns, he imagined that she would think George had been burnt while helping to put out the fire—she knew George that little. She wouldn't know that he couldn't go out to help their father fight a fire, or do anything else for that matter. She was his mother, she should know that—she should be trying to find out why George had changed, why he hardly ever went to school, why he stayed in his room all the time except for meals

31

and didn't say a word to anyone except Bobby. It had been frustrating for Bobby to try to tell his mother that she had to get some help for George. She would always say, "I've done that, I've told him I'd get him some help, but he always just walks away." Bobby felt sorry for his mother. She was so weak.

Bobby opened the windows and turned on the lights before sitting on the bed next to George. The skin of George's arms and neck looked blackened and the burnt areas were oozing fluid.

"Do the burns hurt a lot?"

George made no reply for what seemed like a long time and then said, "Nah, it's nothing, really." The way he said this made Bobby feel that he was now just one of *them* to George. He'd been afraid for some time that he was losing George or that George was losing him.

"The fire wasn't much, just some grass," Bobby said, trying to act as if he were talking to the brother George once was.

"Don't worry about it," George said groggily.

"Sorry, George."

"About what?"

"You know what I'm talking about. Going out there with Dad."

"Bobby, why shouldn't you do what you want to do?"

"But you didn't come with me."

"So what?"

"Don't act dumb," Bobby said.

"When I act dumb, I'm not acting," George said.

Bobby smiled.

"So the fire department came."

"No, the truck wasn't a fire truck. Dad was going crazy in the way he does when he tries to be in charge of everything. You know how he gets. He was trying to put out the fire with an old rusty fire extinguisher—you know, the one in the toolshed. But it wouldn't work, and he didn't want to call the fire department. The whole thing was crazy. He should have called them instead of flagging down a pesticide man to play firemen with him. I don't know why the guy agreed to play that game with him."

Bobby told George that the man who brought the water in his pesticide truck was named Boy. George came to life when he heard this. "If there is a man named Boy," he said, "somewhere there must be his mirror image: a boy named Man. And that boy, already a man, is destined to grow up to be a man who is a generation older than all the other men of his generation. He possesses mature wisdom and will be revered by everyone who meets him or hears about him. The rest of us are stuck in our own generation; we're not a Man-Boy or a Boy-Man, we're just boys who grow up to be men, and there's nothing particularly interesting about that."

George fell silent.

"Why are you stopping?"

"I'm not stopping, I'm just pausing to think."

"Think what?"

"I don't know. If I knew, I'd say it."

"George, are you all right—I mean, the burns?" Bobby said.

"Sure, I'm all right."

"Don't they hurt? They look bad."

"Bobby, things don't hurt if you don't care if they hurt."

The sound of their father's hurried footsteps on the squeaky wooden stairs to the second floor startled George and frightened Bobby as they sat next to one another on George's bed. They girded themselves as the footsteps turned the corner at the top of the stairs and approached the door to George's room. Their father knocked on the half-open door and peered at the two of them as if asking permission to come in, knowing he was entirely unwanted. He then stepped a few feet into the room. His presence on the second floor felt strange to all three of them. Bobby couldn't remember the last time his father had been up there. Maybe never. He half-remembered once, a long time ago, his father using a tall stepladder to replace a burnt-out light bulb in the ceiling light fixture, but he wasn't sure that this had actually happened; it could have been a dream.

Their father's face and arms were streaked with ash in the same way as Bobby's. He surveyed the room as if stepping into a flying saucer. He no doubt noticed the globs of plastic stuck to the fibers of the carpet. There was a pregnant silence. George rose to his feet and stood with his arms crossed against his chest, probably in an effort to conceal the burns.

"George, George …," their father said in a tone of voice that hovered halfway between disappointment and tenderness.

George stood there silently.

"Come here. Let me see what's happened."

Bobby was surprised to see George walk over to where their father was standing.

"It's nothing," George said, which also surprised Bobby.

"No, it's not nothing. Hold out your arms."

George's right forearm was deep red, weeping in places.

"Let's go downstairs to the medicine chest so I can put some ointment on it."

Their father led the small parade down the hallway, down the narrow staircase, through their parents' low-ceilinged, almost completely dark bedroom, and into their parents' bathroom—a small room painted pink, an odd color more suited to a little girl than grown-ups, Bobby had always thought.

Bobby knew from experience that their father went crazy over little things, but when it came to big things, he could be calm, reassuring, even kind. The big things had happened only a few times, so far as Bobby could remember.

Their father pulled open the door to the medicine cabinet, a four-foot-high piece of pink-painted plywood with a tarnished circular chrome handle. Inside were four wooden shelves loaded with prescription pill bottles, tubes of creams and ointments, Band-Aids, a hot water bottle, enema equipment, and other things that Bobby didn't want to look at because it seemed like a private place containing things not meant for his eyes, especially his mother's medical things.

Their mother, as this was happening, made herself scarce. Bobby thought that she might want to let their father do something with them when he wasn't angry, but it might have been that she just didn't know how to respond to emergencies. Their father was good in emergencies. The whole family had to admit that. He knew what to do and did it. Bobby thought his father had learned in the Army how to deal with emergencies, but he had never asked.

Their father washed his hands thoroughly with a bar of soap in the small bathroom sink, like a surgeon, and then sat down on the edge of the tub, motioning to George to sit down beside him. He ran the bathtub faucet until the water was warm and gently washed the burned skin with a washcloth. He lit a match from a matchbook he had in his pocket and held the metal tweezers in the flame for a few seconds. He then carefully removed pieces of burnt plastic; he was good at this. He applied Neosporin with his forefinger to all the red areas and used Q-tips when applying it to the weeping areas. Now and again, he gently turned George's arm or asked him to turn his head a little this way or that so he could get a better look at a particular area. He then sprayed the burned areas with Novocaine, which he said would make the burns hurt less. George's face relaxed as the cool mist fell gently on his skin.

Their father took out a roll of gauze and asked Bobby to run to the kitchen to get the scissors. Bobby appreciated the fact that his father had given him a role in this scene. Before wrapping George's forearm in gauze, their father used his teeth to tear some strips of adhesive tape from the roll, and stuck one end of each to the side of the tub. Maybe he'd been a medic in the Army, Bobby thought. He knew his father had enlisted in the Army during the Depression, two years out of high school, when there was no work available. He wanted to be useful, Bobby's mother told him. Bobby recognized the word *useful* as his father's word because he so often said to George and him, "Make yourself useful." She said he was handsome in his military uniform, at least in photos. They didn't meet until after he got out. She couldn't recall where she'd put the photos. Bobby's father never talked about his time in the Army.

George seemed calmed by the way their father was speaking to him, the way he held George's arm and cradled George's head against his shoulder when washing or applying ointment to the back of his neck. George did not say a word except for an occasional "Okay" in response to his father's asking how he was doing. Bobby had never seen their father be so gentle with either of them. He always seemed not to know, or want to get to know, either George or him. He never asked about what happened at school, or whether they'd liked a movie they'd gone to see, or anything else. He looked, to Bobby, as if he were continually brooding about something, but Bobby had no idea what he was brooding about.

Bobby knew his father sold insurance, but his father never said anything about his work or the people he worked with, or even the place where he worked. Bobby could not remember his father ever smiling, much less laughing. He never showed any warmth that Bobby could remember, which was what made the way he was attending to George that evening so striking. He hadn't questioned either him or George about how the fire began, which Bobby greatly appreciated. It was clear that the fire began in the brush right below the windows of George's room. And he hadn't commented on the rank odor of urine and burnt plastic and shit in George's room. What a strange, impenetrable, unpredictable man their father was, Bobby thought.

PART II

CAROL

SIX

They lived in a town just north of Poughkeepsie. Theirs was one of ten houses in a cul-de-sac from which bay windows protruded from the second floors of the mock Victorians. The thick, dark front lawns were watered at 3:00 a.m. by programmed pop-up sprinklers. To the right of each house was an inclined driveway leading to an ample two-car garage.

Carol's father, Jack, was a tall, broad-shouldered, balding man with a square face and a dimple on his chin. He wore a look of determination on his face as he read *The New York Times* at the breakfast table. He was dressed in a white shirt and striped tie, his suit jacket draped over the back of his chair. Without shifting his gaze from the paper, he drank his orange juice, ate his poached egg, and drank a cup of coffee with cream and sugar. The silence was occasionally cut by the sound of a spoon against the side of a coffee cup. At the table with him were his wife, Phoebe, who sat at the round table without a plate or glass or cup in front of her, and their fourteen-year-old daughter, Carol, who jabbed her spoon into her bowl of cereal once in a while as she read her book. He seemed unaware of the presence of either of them, an acting skill he'd perfected.

Carol, unable to stand the tension any longer, said, "What are you reading, Daddy?"

"A rare thing, very rare. A gas of some sort erupted a few days ago from a lake in Africa and killed dozens of people."

Her mother scoffed simply by exhaling slightly more emphatically than usual, which was sufficient to express her disdain for her husband, a junior high school principal, who would never earn a fraction of what her father and her two brothers did.

At 7:25, Jack rose from the table and said goodbye to his wife, whom he called "Dear," never "Phoebe." Trailing after her father, juggling her bag of books and binders, Carol tripped as she hurried down the back stairs but managed not to fall. The drive to school with her father was her favorite part of the day. She was very proud of him. He was a kind and intelligent man, and strikingly handsome, she thought. They talked about television shows and movies they'd watched together, and what her major would be when she went to college, or a novel they were both reading. They talked about her father's ambition to be selected by the board of supervisors to become superintendent of schools in their district and about her mother's drinking problem. Carol was the only person with whom he talked about what was happening in the family. And yes, she knew all about girls falling in love with their fathers, which, she agreed, does happen sometimes.

The school year had not yet begun, so the drive with her father was the only part of the day they spent alone together outside the house. During the school year, she could drop by the junior high school administration office where he reigned firmly yet compassionately, she thought, and everyone in the school office agreed. He had refused Carol's request to spend the day reading in the school library and drive home with him at the end of his day at school. No students were allowed in the school building before school started because teachers were preparing their rooms for the beginning of classes and needed to feel free to talk honestly among themselves and with him about their ideas and plans and especially their worries about particular students in the upcoming school year.

After her father parked his car in the space reserved for the principal, Carol grabbed her bag of books from the back seat and stood next to the car, looking as dejected as she could manage, but her father was unswerving in his insistence she not be at the school building. Walking home, book bag at her side, she liked the feel of the cool, moist morning air on her face and arms. She enjoyed talking to herself, not knowing and not caring whether she was speaking out loud or speaking to herself in her head. In these "conversations," she talked with Marie Curie or Emma Woodhouse or Jo March. They were her best friends, other than her father and Gillian. But Gillian wouldn't be back until the beginning of school. They'd be ninth graders then.

On arriving home from her walk from school, it wasn't yet 9:30 and the heat of the sun was already gathering strength; the thermometer outside the kitchen window read 82 degrees, and the air was still. Carol climbed the stairs to her room. As she lay on her bed with the door open, she could hear her mother on the phone in the kitchen, speaking in the annoying, high-pitched voice she used when she was gossiping. Carol got up and walked to the head of the stairs where she could hear her mother repeating her usual complaints about her father— "… he lacks ambition … We're stuck in this ghetto for the *nouveau riche* with all of our resources coming from my inheritance … His manhood shriveled up the minute Carol was born."

Carol, sensing the conversation was about to end, walked quietly back to her room. Five minutes later, she heard her mother call from downstairs, "Carol, come here, sweetie. Would you come here just for a minute?"

Carol at first pretended not to hear, but her mother persisted. When she couldn't stand her mother's bleating any longer, Carol stiffly descended the stairs.

"Sweetheart, I'm in the living room," she said, as if Carol didn't know. As Carol entered the room, eyes to the floor, her mother was seated at the far end of the apricot-colored couch that stood in the middle of the room. Two bloated yellow arm-chairs faced the couch across a low wooden coffee table.

Carol flopped down into the armchair farthest from her mother. Though not looking at her, Carol could hear her mother swirling her highball glass, causing the ice cube to tap lightly against the sides.

"Carol, I can hardly see you over there. Have a seat on the couch next to me."

Carol moved to the couch but tucked herself deeply into the pillows as far from her mother as she could get.

"Sweetheart, I know you were listening to me from the top of the stairs."

"No, I wasn't."

"Yes, you were."

"I have no secrets from your father. I've told him to his face everything I said on the phone. I hope it didn't shock you."

"You shouldn't be drinking so early in the day."

"Sweetheart, every grown-up does that. It's not a big deal. Businessmen have two or three drinks in their offices before noon, and then they go out for business lunches where they have two or three more drinks. They have a tray of glasses and bottles of scotch and vodka in their offices to drink with clients and business partners. It makes things more casual, more natural. I'm not making this up. I grew up in a family of successful businessmen. They drink far more than I do."

"Dad doesn't do that."

"He's not a businessman, he's a junior high school principal."

"Dad says you're a drunk," Carol said, realizing only after the words were out of her mouth that she was divulging something he'd said to her in confidence.

"He does no such thing."

"I've heard you arguing in your bedroom, and I've heard him say it to you," Carol lied.

"All parents argue and say things they don't mean."

"Do you know what you look like when you're drunk?" Carol said.

"Sweetie, that hasn't happened in a long time."

"A long time! It happens every day."

"I don't remember the last time it happened."

"It's impossible to talk to someone who lies all the time."

"On honey, let's not be melodramatic."

"You lie to yourself and you believe the lies."

"He's been having an affair for I don't know how long … Oh, I see in your face you didn't know."

"Of course I knew. With Miss Freid, the ninth-grade English teacher," she said, hoping her guess was right.

Carol struggled to get to her feet, but found herself sucked into the flabby couch cushions. Her mother took advantage of the situation by leaning over and grabbing at her wrist. As Carol fought her way out of the suction from the couch and the grip of her mother's hand, she found herself much too close to her mother's face—the cloudy eyes, the smell of alcohol on her breath, the cheeks collapsing into thick jowls, the lurid red of her eyelids, the bags under her eyes loosely rippling downward on each side until they gathered into a rounded layer of fat under her chin that cascaded down her neck. In her mother's animal-like existence, time did not pass—mornings, afternoons, evenings, days, weeks, and years were all the same; there were no beginnings, middles, and ends; there was no next step, no arrivals, no departures.

Carol, having wrestled her way to her feet, turned and walked through the kitchen and out the back door, down to the bottom of the concrete stairs, where she turned sharply and walked into the dark, dank, faintly foul-smelling space under the steps where the metal garbage cans were kept. She took her customary place—her back leaning against the wood siding of the house—and pounded her forehead with the heel of her hand again and again. The voice in her head came at her

43

in a cold, composed tone. *A year ago—ninth grade, wasn't it— you felt virtually certain your father was having an affair with Miss Freid, didn't you? And didn't you take the bus into town and buy at Luckey Platt's a shade of lipstick just like Miss Freid's? And didn't you come home and take from your parents' hamper one of your father's white oxford cloth shirts that he wears to work? And didn't you very carefully apply a little of the lipstick to your lower lip, and after wiping almost all of it off with a tissue, didn't you very softly touch your lip to the collar of the shirt? Though you can't be sure that your mother noticed it when she took the shirts to the cleaner, she's very observant, isn't she?*

Carol slid to the ground, her legs pulled up in front of her. She didn't cry. She wasn't that kind of girl. The pain of the shame and anger burning inside, and the hot piercing pain of the headache, melted into a feeling of calm, profound calm: She was nowhere, no one, floating cloud-like as in a dream.

After a while, as if waking from a sleep so deep that she had to figure out where she was, she recognized the sides of the metal garbage cans not five feet in front of her, which helped her locate herself in the space under the back stairs, and to become aware of the hot pain of the headache and the nausea that was welling up in her. She then awkwardly got to her feet, brushed herself off, and stepped unsteadily out into the glare of the sun, which added explosive force to the pain in her head. Without making a decision to do so, she found herself walking back to the school building, intent on finding some dark corner where she could read a book she'd steal from the library or perhaps simply sleep unnoticed.

SEVEN

Carol dropped her book bag onto the faded black rubber doormat and reached deep into the pocket of her winter coat as she tried to fish out the key to the front door. Before entering the house, Carol stamped her feet to get the snow off her boots. On stepping inside, she was slammed in the face by the familiar scent of alcohol and cigarette smoke.

Carol glanced into the living room, which was lit only by the bit of late afternoon light that managed to find holes in the thick red velour drapes that looked like they belonged in a movie theater. The room was overheated and clammy. Carol's mother was asleep on the couch, half-covered by a blanket, one bare leg protruding toward the floor as if she'd collapsed, head first, face down, onto it. Carol walked through the living room, through a short hallway, and into the kitchen. She opened the cabinet beneath the sink, grabbed a can of air freshener, walked back into the living room and sprayed the room and then her mother from the top of her head to the toes of her protruding foot. Her mother raised her hand from under her blanket and waved Carol away mumbling in a treacly sweet voice, "Don' do that, honey. Can't you see I'm napping. Make yourself a sandwich or something."

"You're grotesque. You stink up the whole house."

"Carol, I wasn't always like this," her mother sighed, squeezing enough air from her lungs to complete the sentence in one breath.

Carol, while straightening up the area around her mother on the couch, reflexively shook off her mother's comment like a dog just in from the rain shaking the water, head to toe, from its body. But she couldn't help admitting that her mother was right, she hadn't always been like this. She'd once been beautiful—exceptionally beautiful, Carol thought. In grammar school, on back-to-school night, she was thrilled by the idea of her teacher meeting her mother, who in the simplest of ways separated herself from the other mothers—a slightly different shade of lipstick, a bracelet that while inexpensive, shone like a star on her wrist, a scarf someone had brought her from Europe that she tied in the most glorious, unassuming knot and wore just the tiniest bit off center. She had thought of her mother as a Christmas tree on which just one ornament hung, but more lovely, more arresting than all of the thickly ornamented trees. And her mother thought Carol was dazzling. They shopped in the least expensive stores as if on a treasure hunt. Her mother had been her best friend. Carol had not spoken those words to herself in many years, but they'd been true. That mother had died years ago. She couldn't wait for this woman to die so she could have her real mother back.

"I was just about to get up. I didn't sleep well last night, so I took a nap. I was just about to get up when I heard you at the door. You okay, sweetheart? Are you all there?"

"Do you really believe you're interested in my life? You do, don't you? Unbelievable."

"Honey, how's the play going?"

"The single performance of the play occurred three weeks ago. You couldn't make it, remember?"

"I forgot. Everybody forgets things."

"You're not everybody, you're a drunk."

"Sweetheart, I'm trying. You have to give me that."

Carol yelled at the top of her lungs, "You're lying there drunk, half on the couch, half on the floor, you actually believe you're trying! Nobody believes you're trying. You never went to rehab or AA or anything. You're way past trying. Your story's over." Carol hated the sound of her own voice—shrill and bitter. She heard herself groveling, and admitted to herself that, at seventeen years old, her story was over, too. Her father had moved out a year and a half ago and was living in an apartment fifteen minutes away by car. He claimed to be living alone, but no man buys flowers for an apartment where he lives by himself.

Her mother, extending her hand in Carol's direction as if to stroke her hair, rolled off the couch with one leg stretched toward the ceiling in a last effort to prevent herself from rolling off onto the floor—a dark comedy if it weren't actually happening. The smell of urine released from her mother's previously covered body assaulted Carol's face like a blow. Her mother's wasted body fell to the floor with a thud, but not before her head hit the side of the glass coffee table.

Carol heard herself screaming, "Mommy!" She was repulsed by the warm odor rising from her mother's body, which was now lying sideways on the carpet facing the couch, her nightgown pulled up to her waist, her wet nylon panties and wrinkled thighs exposed. Carol knelt down and forcefully turned her mother's face upward in an effort to see if the forehead was cut deeply. There was a swelling the size of a silver dollar with a cut of some sort that Carol could hardly see through her mother's matted, dull silver hair.

"Sit on the couch—God, it stinks in here—so I can see how deep the cut is." Carol stooped down and took hold of her mother's bony, loose-skinned upper arms and tried to hoist her up onto the couch, but the dead weight of her mother's body prevented her from getting her past a sitting position on the floor, her back slumped against the couch.

"It seems like only a small cut, but I don't know if you need stitches or something, and I'm not going to make that decision for you. You'll have to do that for yourself. Call a doctor or an ambulance, whatever you like."

"Honey, of course you shouldn't have to make a decision like that. I'll be fine."

"If you say so."

What was happening today was hardly the worst of what Carol had to do as caretaker of her mother's body. There were days when Carol knew immediately from the odor that hit her in the face when she opened the front door of the house that her mother's panties and nightgown would be not only soaked with urine, but also laden with shit that had become smeared over her. This was the most repulsive part of taking care of her mother. On those days, her mother was almost always in an alcoholic haze, hardly herself, hardly anyone. Carol was grateful for this because she loathed the sound of her mother's voice talking at her. She used a soapy washcloth to wipe the shit from down below. She kept her eyes shut and turned her head sharply to the side, holding her breath for as long as she could, then inhaling deeply through her mouth, and then again holding her breath as she scrubbed with the washcloth-covered hand, trying not to give shape in her mind to what her hand was touching.

When she had completed as much of the washing as she could bear, Carol would remove her mother's nightgown and pick up her panties from the floor. Carrying the filthy nightgown and panties between two fingers, she'd climb the stairs to her mother's bathroom, where she'd step on the pedal of the metal hamper and drop the clothing into its open bin. (A housekeeper came for two hours every weekday to do the laundry and tidying up.) She'd then go to her mother's bureau, pick out a fresh nightgown and underwear, and return to the living room, where her mother would be sprawled face-up across

48

the couch wearing only her bra. Carol would then wrestle her unconscious mother into the clean clothes.

Carol came to hate the female body with its layout of orifices, wishing they didn't exist. She wished she had the body of her dolls.

Strangely, on the day her mother cut her head, it wasn't the sight of her mother hitting her head on the coffee table as she fell from the couch, or the sensations involved in cleaning up the excrement, that was most disturbing to Carol, for none of that was a surprise. What most upset her was hearing herself calling out the word *Mommy*.

"I'll meet you in the kitchen in a few minutes, sweetheart. You just go on ahead and I'll join you. I promise."

Carol heard the sound of the words her mother spoke, but not their meanings. The inside of her head didn't feel right. It felt like something was living in there that wasn't her. The feeling was there all the time, but it got better or worse depending on what was happening. It was bad now. She didn't feel steady on her feet as she walked through the kitchen and out the back door, down the concrete steps, back to the place under the stairs where the metal garbage cans stood, almost as if they were solemnly waiting for the dark ceremony to begin.

EIGHT

When Carol's father had told her he would hire some-one to take care of her mother, should Carol "want to pursue postgraduate studies," and he would be glad to pay for her tuition and living expenses, she had been able to give him only one-word responses (in the affirmative). She had asked him for almost five years to hire a full-time attendant for her mother or have her put in a nursing home. And what was going on when he used the phrase "should you want to pursue postgraduate studies," when he knew she had wanted to go to graduate school in English practically from the time she learned to speak? They'd dreamt of that day together for years during their chats as he drove her to school when she was a child.

In fact, he hadn't hired anyone to tend to her mother; he preferred to keep his wife's alcoholic degeneration—not to mention his long-standing affair with an English teacher—a secret from everyone outside the family, because any hint of such behavior would squash any chance he had of becoming superintendent of schools.

He left it to Carol to buy food and other supplies for her mother and to take care of her in every other way in exchange for a generous "allowance"—a euphemism for as much money as she wanted. Carol, before moving into a small apartment of her own not far from the campus of the regional branch of the state university, had bought a portable toilet for her mother and trained her mother to use it, which her mother was able do some of the time. On her daily visits, Carol peeled off her mother's wet nightgown and panties, and washed the urine and feces from her mother's body, working her way down from her mother's hips and buttocks to the parts of her body down there that repulsed her. She would empty the portable toilet into the toilet in the laundry room, move the laundry from the washer to the dryer, put the dirty laundry in the washer, and then return to her apartment, where she stood under a hot shower scrubbing the skin all over her body as hard as she could, though she could never completely rid herself of the stench of her mother.

He'd used her. He'd taken advantage of the fact that for some reason she'd continued to look after her mother long after any sane person would have. He must have been stunned by his good fortune that his daughter was unable to leave her mother, and unable even to threaten to expose him for the way he was managing his family or for his affair with the English teacher.

Carol could not explain to herself why she'd agreed to this arrangement, or why she continued to agree to it for the three years it took her to complete her undergraduate degree in English. During the days and weeks after he told her he would hire someone to care for her mother, she'd tortured herself with questions: Why was he releasing her now? Why should she believe he would hire an attendant? Was she lying to herself and participating in killing her mother? Would she be horrified if her mother died alone of neglect, or would she feel vast relief? She didn't have answers to any of these questions. What she wished for, most of all, was to be able not to care in the slightest what the answers to these questions might be.

On the day she left Poughkeepsie for graduate school, it would have been simpler to take the taxi directly from her apartment to the bus station. Instead she asked the driver to take her to her mother's house and wait outside for a few minutes. She knew her mother would be asleep on the couch, though every time she entered her mother's house she half expected to find her mother had died by choking on her own vomit. She was greeted by the familiar odor and overheated air. Her mother always felt cold and kept the heat on day and night, even in the summer. Carol stared at the sharp edges of her mother's emaciated body, which lay facing the back cushions of the couch. A sheet covered her shins and feet. The house was silent except for the sound of her mother snoring and occasionally clearing her throat as if she were about to say something. After gazing at the figure on the couch, Carol turned and stepped out of the house, closing the door behind her for the last time in her life.

The bus from Poughkeepsie to Buffalo stopped to pick up and drop off passengers at bus stops or bus terminals every hour or so. Carol made the seat beside her as unappealing as possible, strewing it with Cheese-It crumbs, a half-empty pack of cigarettes (though she didn't smoke), and Drumstick ice cream cone wrappers glistening with brown streaks of chocolate that looked for all the world like shit. When the bus was full, she had no choice but to allow the seat to be taken, but even so, she either pretended to be asleep or, better yet, feigned illness by sneezing and coughing, flaunting a high possibility of contagion. Displays of this sort were more effective with women than with men. Women seemed not to want to be sullied by her and coiled themselves into a dense, compact ball that served to contract the surface area vulnerable to contamination by her, but now and again there was a woman who talked continuously, seeming to know that Carol was awake even while her eyes were closed, her head leaning against the window, and her mouth emitting a sputtering snore. The men and boys usually kept to themselves, acting as if she weren't there. But among the boys and men who wanted to talk, sexual appetite was the common denominator among them. They acted as if they were on a first date at a drive-in movie, as if she would find them cool or handsome or intelligent or worldly or blessed with some other trait that would distract her and themselves from the fact that they were on a bus, not a plane or even a train, and that their desirability was solely a fiction they'd invented and could even at times get themselves to believe. She imagined they would protect themselves from her disdain by saying to themselves that she must be frigid, a term men use for women who don't go around trying to get fucked by the first man they meet on a bus. One man her father's age pushed his face across the two-inch space separating his seat cushion from hers and talked at her with a raspy deep voice, trying to force her to make eye contact with him. On feeling the fetid moisture of his saliva-saturated breath on her cheek, she put her face down in her lap and said, "I'm sorry, I think I'm going to vomit."

Carol spent the night at a motel in Buffalo—one of those archetypal single-story places with a broken neon sign reading Vacancy and a row of twenty rooms with cars parked in front of a half-dozen of them and an empty swimming pool in back—before taking another bus on the final leg of the trip the next morning, bound for the station that she had been told was closest to campus.

Carol stepped down the stairs at the front of the bus into blinding sunlight. She surveyed the terrain through squinted eyes, trying to get a sense of the place where she might be living for the next five years. The terrain was dismally flat as she looked east over the railroad tracks at what appeared to be factories and warehouses, possibly abandoned, with nothing and no one moving. She waited as the other passengers pulled out their suitcases, most of which were torn and overstuffed, some held together by duct tape. When the others had rushed off as if late for a connecting bus or to find a family member to drive them home, she pulled her faded maroon duffel bag out of the empty hold as if delivering the last of quintuplets hidden in the far corner of the birth canal.

In the terminal, her constricted pupils rendered her practically blind, a sensation she found interesting. Even if only for a few moments, she could feel what it must be like to depend almost entirely on her other senses. She noticed a low hum of people speaking without discernible words, the clicking of heels against concrete or tile floors, the relatively cool air that seemed on the brink of losing its battle with the heat of the day, and the odor of sweat and mold. As her eyes adjusted to the dim light, she saw the long hallway of a surprisingly ornate building with high ceilings and walls of mosaic tiles. It must once have been the railroad station of a prosperous region.

As she made her way to the doors at the back of the building, Carol passed benches on which people—probably adults, perhaps teenagers—were stretched out, here and there, legs forward, a fully stuffed black plastic garbage bag tucked under their legs, as if they were members of a platoon of soldiers awaiting orders that would never come. On the wall at the end of the terminal there was a map of the area on which the "You are here" arrow had been scraped off, and in its place was written in black marker, "Nowhere Man."

Outside the back of the terminal stood a curb that stretched some thirty or forty yards, partially shaded by a corrugated, faded green plastic overhang. Two taxis were parked at the far left end, their windshields reflecting the bright sunlight, making it impossible to see whether there were drivers in the cars.

It was well before noon so Carol decided to walk to campus. She set out in the direction indicated on a sign bearing the university seal. She walked along a narrow, worn path on the right-hand shoulder of the two-lane road. It was a warm, dry day at the beginning of September. Carol was briefly awoken from the daze in which she was enfolded when the occasional car or truck roared past, leaving in its trail tiny particles of dirt swirling in a thin blue-gray cloud of exhaust. It was a relief to be able to reduce herself to the sound and sensation of the crunch of pebbles underfoot, the aching of her shoulders, and the feel of thick saliva caked on the edges of her mouth.

A pickup truck slowed as it approached Carol from behind. A man, whose salt-and-pepper beard she saw out of the corner of her eye, yelled across the passenger seat through the open window, "Want a ride, girl?"

Without turning her head, as if flicking a fly off her arm, she said, "Fuck off." He drove on.

As mid-day turned into mid-afternoon, Carol began to have the uneasy feeling that she may have taken the wrong road. Her back and legs were on the verge of collapsing under the weight of the duffel bag. She could feel blisters forming on the soles of her feet in the ill-fitting boots she'd bought at an army-navy store. No longer able to lose herself in thought, she began chastising herself for engaging in the charade of the strong, independent woman. Who's the audience for this pathetic performance, she wondered.

Quickly these thoughts became dominated by a severe woman's voice calling her a pretentious fraud, a disgusting creature who had never had a friend in her life and whom no one would want as a roommate. As the voice in her head became louder, Carol lost track of the direction in which she was headed. Could she have turned around without realizing it, now heading back to the bus station? She considered sitting down by the side of the road, but rejected the idea because she'd probably be hit by a car or truck. The right shoulder of the road was narrow and dropped off precipitously into a deep gulley; the left shoulder rose abruptly into a steep hillside packed with evergreens and birches.

She continued walking until she sighted on the other side of the road, a few hundred yards ahead, a paved surface that appeared to be a parking area in front of a house or business tucked back from the road. As she approached, she could see that the area was the front of a gas station. There was a man stooped down with his back to her, placing cans of what she guessed was motor oil on the shelves of a rack that stood on the near side of the single gas pump. When she was about ten years old, her father had taught her how to use a dipstick to check the oil of their car. The memory filled her with sadness. That man no longer existed.

"You lost?"

Having momentarily lost track of where she was, Carol was startled by the man's voice. She let her duffel bag flop to the ground, not caring where it landed or how she appeared to him.

"Is there a blood bank around here?" she said.

"You making a deposit or a withdrawal?"

"What are you talking about?"

"I've done it once or twice for the money and the food— orange juice, cookies, sometimes sandwiches if you're lucky," he said in a tone of voice she couldn't figure out.

"Done what?" she said.

"Given blood at a blood bank."

"What are you talking about?" she said with annoyance.

"You're the one who asked if there's a blood bank around here."

She became even more confused by his talk about blood bank deposits, withdrawals, cookies, and sandwiches. She tried to get her bearings by slowly, deliberately examining the place and the man she'd happened upon: a gas station selling Regal Gas, a brand she'd never heard of, run by a guy several years older than she, mid-twenties maybe, not a dangerous man, she thought, with longish but not wild, light brown hair, whose face was covered with sweat that ran down into his eyes, causing him to rub them with the back of his hand. About thirty feet behind the pump was a small office-like structure with a glass door and a large window to its left. To the right of the office was a long building about ten feet taller than the office, fronted by a pair of large glass-paned garage doors. Seven or eight rather beat-up cars were parked in a row at right angles to the garage.

"Where am I?"

"It depends on where you're going."

"I'm sorry if I confused you by what I asked, but please don't make fun of me. Where is this place?"

"I thought you were joking with me, but you weren't. You're looking for the university, right?"

"Yes, that's right."

"Could we start over again?" he said.

"How far is the university from here?"

"It's 2.2 miles, but it's uphill, so it's a tough walk, specially with that duffel bag of yours. There's a fridge in the office where there's cold sodas. Can I get you one?"

"Yes, I'd like that."

He brought a Dr. Pepper out to her. By this time she'd moved her duffel bag into the shade just outside the office.

"Would you like to sit down inside the office while you drink that? I'll leave you to yourself in there, unless you'd like some company."

"I'd like some company," she heard herself say, though that wasn't entirely true.

He opened the door, a glass door with a wooden sash, its red paint flaking.

Below the dust-covered windows on the front and on both sides of the room were wooden benches with blue cloth pads on them. A desk with an adding machine and cash register stood to her right.

"Air conditioning?" he asked, again startling Carol.

"Sure," she said, dissembling ease.

As the man knelt in front of the air conditioner in the wall under the window opposite the desk, he said, with his back to her, "My name's Robert, by the way—Robert Renfro, but my friends call me Robert."

She smiled. "I'm Madeline Townsend." Such a strange feeling to change your name, to become someone else, unplanned, in the space of a fraction of a second. Not a random name—Madeline was the name of her grandmother, her father's mother, who died when she was eight. She hadn't known her very well and had only a few memories of her that were hard to distinguish from photos she'd seen. Her grandmother had painted still-life paintings, one of which hung on a wall in the living room of her mother's house, and another on the wall at the side of the staircase to the second floor. She liked the name Madeline, which she associated not only with her grandmother, but also with the French storybook character Madeline, and with Proust's famous cookie. It's the name of a woman to be taken seriously, she thought—a solid person, a little strange for someone who isn't old, but so much better than Carol. She'd never felt like a Carol. Carol sounded like the name of a cheerleader.

Robert sat quietly at the desk while Carol, now Madeline, sitting on the bench with her head leaning back on the window facing the gas pump, fell asleep for most of an hour. Watching her felt to Robert like watching a small child deep in sleep. A trusting thing to do, he thought. The less intense, less bleaching light of the late afternoon sun rendered the leaves of the ginkgo trees across the street a vibrant hue, the color of ripe apricots, of rich orange shining through the yellow surface, which Robert found magnificent.

Concerned that this girl might need to register at the university before the end of the afternoon, he stood over her and quietly said, "You on your way to the university?"

As she opened her eyes, she found the face of a man, his body not three feet from hers.

"It's five-twenty. If you're going to register and get your room assignment, you'd better get going. They close at six. I'll drive you."

"Did you already tell me who you are and I've forgotten?" she said, getting to her feet awkwardly.

"Yes, my name's Robert."

"And who did you say you are?"

"I didn't say. I work here at this gas station."

"And what do you do here … Oh forget it. It doesn't really matter."

"Aren't you going to the university?"

"I suppose so?"

"You suppose?"

"Yeah, my heart's not really in it if you want to know the truth … But why would you want to know the truth?"

"I'd be interested in the truth. If you haven't noticed, there's not much else of interest going on around here."

"I don't know the truth, and I'm not much interested in finding out. 'The truth' is invariably bad."

"I'll drive you."

"You don't have to drive me."

"You're not going to make it up that hill on foot."

"Why would you go out of your way like that?"

"Because I want to."

"I guess that's a good reason … You know a lot about how it works there, at the university."

"You mean you didn't think I'm the sort who goes to a university."

"No—well, yes, I guess I didn't. What are you doing working at this gas station?"

"To tell you the truth, I sometimes wake up in the morning, look around, not fully awake, and say to myself, 'How'd you end up working at a gas station?'"

Madeline didn't know what to make of this man who was probably twenty-six or twenty-seven, had a quiet manner, and seemed intelligent. So why did she say that horrible thing to him? She *was* surprised that he knew anything about the university up the road; she *did* think "He's not that sort"—a gas station attendant, not of the social class that goes to university. He didn't deserve that—"He didn't," the voice in her head intoned.

"I'd appreciate it if you'd give me a lift up there."

PART III

MADELINE AND ROBERT

Madeline was still groggy from her nap in the gas station's office. The air had cooled markedly. Robert's car was a weathered silver. More than weathered, beat up: rust along the metal under the door on her side, the paint so thin the silver had given way to gray, and the radio antenna snapped off.

Pulling on the handle of the passenger-side door, Madeline leaned back, trying to open it, but it wouldn't budge. Not wanting to ask for help, she yanked hard, which caused her to take an awkward step back as the car door finally opened. On regaining her footing, she stepped toward the car again, only to be met by warm air saturated by an odor of old sneakers. She looked through the interior of the car at the gas station attendant—she'd again forgotten his name—who was now leaning across the driver's seat to the passenger side, tossing empty soda bottles, broken sunglasses, and a crumpled T-shirt into the back seat.

"Sorry about the mess."

"I've seen worse."

The steep, tortuous road leveled off as it entered the south edge of the campus. Madeline watched men in dull blue jumpsuits rolling dollies stacked with wooden crates from the rear of trucks backed up to a loading dock. She caught a glimpse of the interior of a warehouse, a cavern, into and out of which the men walked methodically, silently, like aliens stocking a spaceship with enough food for a century-long journey.

Madeline felt impatient with Robert for driving at the speed of a funeral hearse. Her gaze slid smoothly into alleys, over the surface of cyclone fencing fitted with white metal signs announcing High Voltage, into the tidy recess of a parking lot in which a dozen or so motorized carts were nestled next to one another like sleeping infants in their bassinettes, and then past a dull-orange brick building on which a hand-painted sign read ROTC, a makeshift arrow drawn under the black letters.

Madeline remained silent as Robert took the service road around the campus. When the soft rocking movement of the car and the murmur of the engine ceased, Madeline woke gently from her half-sleep in the warm, late-summer air. As she focused her eyes, she found that they were in a parking lot empty, except for three cars parked under a tree at the far end that looked like tired animals standing flank-to-flank, heads down, drinking at a waterhole, while the sun hung heavily in the western sky. As she located herself and realized whom she was with and why she was there, a wave of thick acidic liquid rose from her stomach into her throat and mouth, a not unfamiliar sensation for her.

"The registrar's office closes at six, and it's twenty of." He seemed to care more about beating the clock than she did, which puzzled her.

Robert didn't bother locking the car before starting to walk briskly across the road and up the broad flight of stairs to the imposing glass entrance doors that stood between two large columns feigning august stature and a long history. Inside the doors was a high-ceilinged room, the floor dappled with sunlight shining through a row of cathedral-like windows that rose on both sides of the hall. On Madeline's right stood a string of wooden tables strewn with sheets of paper that many students, at one time during the day, must have been nervously poring over. The room was empty now.

Sitting behind one of several desks on the left side of the hall, a chinless, middle-aged woman studiously ignored them.

"Madeline, have you filled out the paperwork they sent you?"

"I don't think I want to do this," Madeline said, looking vaguely in Robert's direction.

"You don't want to do what?"

"I don't want to do whatever you call what they're doing here. I'm not going to sign up for anything right now. I need time."

"Time for what?"

"Time, just time. Let's get out of here … please."

"Sure, if that's what you want. You know you won't have a room assignment for tonight."

"What am I going to do with a room assignment?"

"That's where you live when you go to school here."

She liked his sarcasm.

Once uncomfortably back in the car, they both sat staring forward as if waiting for the previews at a drive-in movie.

"You've been very nice to me, and I don't want to impose on you any further. Would you please tell me where there's a pay phone so I can call a taxi?"

"There's one in the building we were just in, but it would be easier to call from the office phone at the gas station."

Madeline turned and looked at him. "I'm sorry to say, I've forgotten your name again. Would you mind telling me one last time?"

"It's Robert."

"Robert, you've been very good to me and I've just refused to do what I asked you to help me do. I really don't want to trouble you any more. My mess of a life is my problem, not yours."

"Well, you've seen the important work I do—stacking oil cans on a rack next to a gas pump. Believe me when I say I'm glad to do whatever you like, and it doesn't matter to me if you change your mind about—or never decide—what you want to do."

"I'd like to just sit here in the car for a few minutes, if that's all right."

They were quiet for some time before Madeline said, "I'm not usually this way. Well, I am, but I'm usually able to keep it hidden. This may be hard for you to believe, given what you've seen of me, but I'm usually the one in charge, the one who takes care of things. I go to school, do well there, I shop, I prepare food, though I wouldn't call it cooking, I call the plumber if there's a leak or a clog, and I arrange to be home right after classes to meet the heater repairman. My father moved out a couple of years ago … Jesus Christ, what am I doing telling you about my father and the plumber? I'm just someone who happened to stop at your gas station lugging a duffel bag, asking directions to a blood bank. It's ridiculous."

"First of all, it's not *my* gas station. I work there, but working there isn't my life … And you didn't just stop at the gas station, I stopped you … because I wanted to meet you. That's not like me, to stop a girl to talk to her."

He fumbled with his keys and started up the car. "Would you like to get something to eat while you decide what you want to do?"

"I'd like that very much."

Madeline, glancing at her watch, was stunned to see that it was almost 7:00.

Robert drove out of the main entrance of the university and turned right onto a narrow road that ran down a hill into the town, a colonial-looking place with a large rectangular green bordered by businesses catering to university students: bookstores, a bank, coffee shops, an inn fronted by a sign made of distressed wood meant to give an "Olde English" impression.

Without telling Madeline where they were going—she didn't care and he knew it—Robert drove along a wide two-lane road, past a shopping mall and a string of car dealerships, to the interstate.

They drove for about ten minutes during which Madeline, as she had as a little girl when driving with her father at this time of year, watched the oaks, maples, aspens, and birches parade past her window in their regal cloaks and crowns of gold and yellow and pink. She was jolted out of her half-sleep by a lurid red neon sign on the roof of an aluminum-sided building ahead of them. The sign read simply DINER, as if to say, "What else do you need to know?" Robert took the next exit. A single dusty big rig was parked facing the diner, like an enormous loyal dog sitting on its belly, eyes forward, front paws planted on the ground, giving its owner time to eat. Eight or nine cars were parked here and there in the parking lot.

Robert held open the glass door of the diner for Madeline. She stepped past him into a space where she was met by a cigarette machine standing heavily against the wall facing her. To its right, screwed to the wall, was its diminutive companion, a pay phone from which dangled on a tarnished wire a thick phone book, stripped of its front and back covers as if having been skinned. To her left, a second glass door opened into the tunnel-like interior of the diner, which was illuminated by light panels on the ceiling that seemed to paint everything they touched with a thin coat of bright white paint.

She followed Robert down the aisle that ran between the burgundy vinyl banquettes on the left, and on the right, the counter into which was tucked a long row of round seats on metal poles, covered with the same burgundy vinyl. Madeline felt as if she were walking onto a film set. She hoped Robert saw the place as she did but doubted he had any such sensibility, and immediately thought that she was a real bitch for thinking that.

There were people seated at all but three or four of the banquettes; a half dozen men were seated at the counter, most of whom were wearing frayed caps with a logo above the bill.

Madeline and Robert slid into opposite sides of one of the banquettes close to the opening in the counter through which the waitresses, in their heavily starched pink uniforms, came and went as they gave the cooks the orders and picked up the plates of food waiting on the stainless steel ledge under orange heat lamps.

Robert looked hard at Madeline across the table. "I eat here a lot. I don't like eating by myself … Don't look at me that way."

"What way?"

"You're trying to figure me out … Don't … You'll never get it right."

"No, I'm not."

"I see the look in your eye. This place is a time warp … I know that … They mean it to be … and I like it this way … This place is home for me. The people here are as close as I have to a family."

"It is true that I was trying to imagine how this place figures into your life. I like it. It has a friendly feel to it." But in truth, she didn't like it much. The place seemed to be aging badly; the vinyl on the seats and banquettes was worn and beginning to crack, and the low, straight ceiling made the place feel like a submarine, particularly now that the windows were black.

The silence that hung between them was filled by the sound of the voices of a waitress engaged in good-natured banter with some regulars and the sound of another waitress's voice yelling orders to the cooks in diner shorthand over the clank and sizzle coming from the kitchen. Though not charmed by the ambiance of this place, Madeline had sense enough to know that this man was entrusting her with something important to him.

"I'm embarrassed to say I have my dinner here a few nights every week."

"Don't be embarrassed. What can be bad about feeling at home somewhere? I've never had that feeling anywhere," which wasn't true, but she'd stopped caring about what was true and what wasn't.

"The food here's pretty good, not great, but …"

"Please don't worry about me."

Waitresses came by carrying trays loaded with dishes, seemingly effortlessly, as if the trays were extensions of their arms. Each gave Robert a knowing smile, to which he responded by shaking his head or rolling his eyes or giving a smile consisting of the slightest upturn of a corner of his mouth.

Both Robert and Madeline were exhausted by the task of conversing with a stranger who was genuinely strange. Strangeness was interesting, at times exciting, but always tiring.

The sound of a deep and raspy woman's voice brought both Robert and Madeline out of their torpor. Standing above them was a tall skinny woman in her pale pink uniform with a nametag that read "AUDREY." She looked about fifty and was wearing lipstick too dark for her complexion, but right for her role in this place, Madeline thought.

"Robert, are you going to introduce me?"

"Audrey, of course I'm going to introduce you, but …"

"But what? I'll behave," said Audrey.

"Audrey, this is Madeline, who I just met today. She's going to go to the university here. And Madeline, this is Audrey, who is one of the kindest people I've ever known."

"Robert, don't go telling stories."

"I'm sorry, but I have to tell the truth."

Audrey laughed, which revealed a black space in the bottom left portion of her mouth where a tooth was missing.

"Madeline, a lot of men come through here, but none at all like this gentleman. We get quite a few ivory-tower types from

71

the university and you can't get so much as a smile or a 'Good morning' out of them. This man's a prize."

Audrey took Madeline's order and then said, "Robert, you'll have the usual, am I right?"

He blushed as he nodded.

After Audrey left, Robert said, "She's a very good person. She's never had children, and I've never had a mother."

Madeline looked Robert in the eye and said, "I hope it's all right if I say you're well loved here." Madeline was afraid Robert wouldn't take this as a compliment. She knew it was very difficult for people to hear warmth in her voice, even when she genuinely felt it, as she did now.

After they finished dinner, Robert looked at his watch and said, "It's getting late. I could take you to a motel or the inn on the town square, which is very nice, but you're welcome to spend the night at the house where I live behind the gas station and you can take your time thinking about what you want to do about registering for classes. Do me a favor and don't take this invitation in the wrong way. Sleeping together's not gonna happen. I'll sleep on the couch and you can have the bedroom with clean sheets that I'll put on it."

Madeline replied, "Before I can make up my mind about your invitation, I have to ask you something."

"What's that?"

"Are you a serial killer, a rapist, or a psychopath?"

Robert smiled broadly and said, "Do I have to choose only one?"

TEN

Madeline tried to hide her fear as Robert drove the final part of the trip back to the gas station—the steep, twisting road down from the campus. The road seemed to melt into thick woods on the right and a gulley on the left. The headlight beams created shadows that squirmed among the trees and bushes. It was past 9:00 the last time Madeline checked her watch, which she had a habit of doing frequently.

Robert parked the car at the left side of the gas station where an industrial-looking, bright white light in a metal cage hung coldly above a door on which there was a red sign with Restroom engraved in white letters. Moths circled the light. The still-warm night air pulsed with the sound of crickets. This was far more nature than Madeline was used to. She watched Robert make his way around to the trunk of the car. He seemed to occupy a world altogether different from hers—less empty, less insular, but she couldn't be sure of that. She couldn't be sure of anything.

After pulling her duffel bag from the trunk, Robert walked briskly to the side of the car where Madeline was standing.

"Would you mind staying here for a couple of minutes? I'd like to straighten things up a little."

"I'll be fine here. Take your time," she said, wondering what he had inside that he was trying to hide.

After some time—five minutes, ten, twenty, who knew?—Robert emerged from the darkness, startling Madeline, who was standing next to the car with her hand on its roof.

Madeline, using the flashlight Robert had brought, followed him along the path from the rear of the gas station to the house, which she imagined to be either a shed-like place or a first cousin to the gas station office.

The path consisted of irregularly shaped slate slabs, separated from one another by a few inches of dried mud. She stopped and raised her eyes to a house dimly visible about twenty yards ahead. It was so vastly different from what she'd expected that it felt unreal, like an image in a dream. The house had the look of a conventional, relatively small, middle-class, suburban ranch house—complete with a front door flanked on the left by a single window and on the right by two windows, all three of which were now aglow from within.

Robert looked back at Madeline, surprised to find her standing still, staring at the house as if discourteously gawking at a handicapped person, finding him a curiosity.

"What did you expect?" he said.

"A makeshift shed, to tell you the truth."

She could see him wince and regretted having told the truth.

Robert said defensively, "I'm told the house was built about twenty years ago, just after the war. When it was built, it was tucked away in the woods with a driveway that ran through the trees, which made it impossible to see from the road. A very quiet and peaceful place. My boss or someone he works for, I don't know which, bought the land to put in a filling station and auto repair service that would be the most convenient place for university students, faculty, and employees to buy their gas and service their cars. This worked well for almost ten years until the interstate was built, and then companies like Esso and Mobil built larger, more convenient

74

gas stations that sold cheaper gas. The auto repair part of the business here keeps it going. Why am I giving you the history of gas stations?"

"It's a good story, a story of chance always having the deciding vote."

"Thanks for turning the mundane into the mythic."

"Any time."

"Well, to complete the saga, after I'd been working here for a while, I asked my boss if I could live in it, and he said, 'Why not, it's just sitting there empty, but it's a dump.' I'd never been in it and when I took a look, I saw that he was right—the place was falling apart and had a foul odor. He agreed to pay for materials if I didn't charge him for labor. In the past I'd worked three or four summers for a contractor who built tract housing, so I knew some carpentry, sheetrocking, taping, plumbing, pouring concrete slabs ... Sorry, I don't mean to bore you."

"Please don't do that."

"Do what?"

"Tell me what I'm feeling."

"So what would you like?"

"I'd like to hear what you did with the house."

"Are you sure?"

"You're doing it again."

"I dug out the back of the house where dirt had slid down from the hill and had piled up above the cinderblock foundation. It was rotting the wood facing and the plywood in back, which made the interior a breeding ground for mold of ten different colors. I built a retaining wall to hold back the dirt from the hill. I replaced the rotten wood with cinderblock, removed the old crumbling roof and put on a new one, opened the walls inside because the plumbing and electricity had been sloppily done, taped and sheetrocked where I'd opened the walls and where the mold had dug in deep, and painted the exterior and interior." Robert then sang (badly), "And he polished up the handle on the big front door!"

Now that he was standing only a foot or so in front of her and looking down from more than a foot above her, Madeline noticed for the first time how tall Robert was.

"I should install a flood light for this path, but I'm the only one who uses it and I know it like the palm of my hand—probably better."

On entering the house, Madeline felt, to her surprise, as if she were entering a private space where someone lived, not a place where someone hid. It was so unlike the house she'd grown up in, where for the past decade the bitterness and chaos and despair spread a film of filth over everything and everyone inside it. Robert's place was private in another way that she didn't have a name for. He didn't rush her as she took a few steps into the house and carefully surveyed it. It wasn't a conventionally orderly interior, she thought, but a type of order was unmistakably present. There was artwork on every wall, every table, and on most of the floor space, with the exception of pathways that allowed passage to the walls and doors and chairs and couch and central table. Paintings were attached to the walls by thumbtacks, one row of paintings over another, and the heavier objects must have been attached to the walls by nails or bolts. Diagonally crossing the room hung a clothes-line to which were attached by wooden clothespins paintings that seemed to be drying.

The house itself was cramped. To her left was a simple kitchen area, in front of her a closed door, and to her right the "living room," in the middle of which was an ample table under a large light fixture that hung from the ceiling.

She took a step back, trying to take it all in, but found she couldn't do it. There was too much to take in all at once. Robert watched Madeline's facial expression as she scanned the room.

On a table just to her right stood a curved piece of blonde wood, about eight or ten inches tall, to which a shiny, chrome-plated triangular piece of metal was attached. She didn't like or dislike it; she just didn't know what to make of it.

Robert said about the piece on which Madeline's gaze was fixed, "It's called assemblage, which ..."

"I know that. It's what Joseph Cornell did," she said, feeling like a schoolgirl know-it-all. Attempting to recover, she asked, "What's it made of?"

"The wood is the curve of the back of an old chair I found, and the chrome is refuse from an office building in which piece like this must have been some part of the structure of the place."

"Where do you get this stuff?"

"Mostly at the county junk yard. They don't like scavengers trawling the place for things to sell, but I've gotten to know the guys who work there, and they seem to genuinely enjoy seeing the things I make with junk—I bring some of the sculptures to show them what I've made. They have a good eye for what works and what's contrived in my sculptures. They're connoisseurs of junk. I gave them a couple of pieces I made that they've bolted to the walls of their small office.

"I don't put anything of mine in the office of the service station. No one here knows I do this sort of thing; they're very respectful of my privacy. No one's been back here except the boss, who's been inside but doesn't give a damn about anything but the improvements I've made to the house. I hang things up and put things out on tables and chairs and on the floor, just to see where I've been."

"They're good. They're really good," she said. She didn't know what else to say.

"That's nice of you to say."

"I'm honored you've let me see the things you make."

"I hadn't thought about how I'd feel ahead of time ... I hadn't expected to feel so ... naked," he said. "A confession: the 'straightening up' I did was actually just taking a few minutes to prepare myself to have you see what's in here."

"I'm sorry I've made you feel that way ... We've been apologizing to each other a lot, like bad dancers who keep stepping on one another's feet."

"My feet don't hurt," he said with his half smile that Madeline had begun to like. She walked deeper into the room.

"Would you mind telling me about what you're working on, the paintings on the work table—is that the right word for it?—over there." The table itself seemed like a work of art in its own right, with its neatly arranged paints in tubes, small bottles filled with what looked like intensely colored paint, jars in which brushes were standing in a murky liquid, sketch pads of different sizes, and several watercolor paintings on slightly lumpy paper.

"The painting I'm working on now is the only one I won't tell you about. I'll tell you about any of the others, if you like."

"What about the one over here, the first one I saw when I walked in the front door—is that all right?"

As though they were a museum docent and a visitor, they walked over to the wall where the three-foot-by-four-foot canvas hung and stood directly in front of it. "I did that with acrylic paint with a brush and a roller. You can see the buildup of paint here made by the edges of the roller. Acrylic paint dries very quickly, so you have to do it in sections of a square foot or two at a time, in bursts lasting twenty or thirty seconds. Stop me when you've heard enough."

"No, keep going. I've never heard an artist talk about their work."

"I'm not being falsely modest when I say that I haven't yet earned the right to be called an artist. I'll know when I reach that point, but I'm not there yet."

"That's ridiculous, of course you're an artist," said Madeline.

"I'm learning how to draw and paint, but what I like most now is making things, like the sculpture you saw, by putting together seemingly useless objects. My eye is always drawn to fallen branches along the road that have knots or twists that make them look like an animal or a human face, and to piles of discarded stuff in front of the dorms at the end of the school year. I fill the trunk of my car with broken record players, floor lamps, photographs, even some torn and worn-out clothes. I draw the line at underwear—that's out of bounds, even for me."

"I'm glad to hear that."

"Over here, in this corner, is something of a pantheon of my gods: photographs of the artists I most respect. You'll recognize them. This is Joseph Cornell, late in life. He spent most of his life taking care of his younger brother with cerebral palsy. The woman is Louise Nevelson in an outrageous hat, and over here is Robert Rauschenberg.

"Actually, the artists I have the greatest affection for are the art professors I've had at the university. None of them is famous or has even been represented by a gallery. They continue, even now, to allow me to work in the school studios. The ventilation in this house isn't sufficient for some of the materials I work with. They let me audit art history classes. They've been like parents to me as well as teachers."

"Like Audrey."

"That's right."

"You're a complicated man, Robert Renfro, and I mean that as a compliment." This she did mean.

"Thanks, but I don't know what kind of man I am. I'm a guy who completed a degree in fine arts and now works in a gas station."

"You've made a very nice place for yourself and your art here. I like it."

"I have to open up the gas station at seven every morning but Sunday, so let me show you the bedroom where you'll sleep. I'll get some fresh sheets for you. I'll sleep on the couch, which is very comfortable."

"I know this will sound outlandishly presumptuous," Madeline said hesitantly, "but would you mind letting me sleep on the couch? I'd be so uneasy sleeping in the bed of a man I hardly know that I wouldn't be able to sleep. And, on top of that, I'd like to spend some time with your artwork."

"If you're sure."

"I'm sure."

"The bathroom's right over there," he said, pointing to a door hidden among the paintings on the wall they were facing.

When Madeline finally crawled under the blanket Robert had laid out over the couch, she decided not to turn out the table lamp that stood just above her head. She didn't feel like sleeping. It felt luxurious to have all the time she wanted to wrap herself in the contents of this room. She thought that if she were more flirtatious, she would have said to Robert, "I want to sleep with your artwork," but flirting was something she didn't do, something she didn't know how to do.

Sounds from the kitchen woke Madeline the next morning, a Sunday morning, so the gas station was closed. It was already close to nine. She had slept in what she'd been wearing. Taking a bag of toiletries from her duffel, she quickly brushed her teeth and did what she could with her hair, which looked greasy in the mirror over the sink. Robert offered to prepare breakfast for her. She said she'd like to get registration over with and asked if he'd mind driving her to the administration building. She hoped he wouldn't feel that she'd simply used him as a free motel, but she was so frightened that she'd again be unable to make herself register that she felt a pressing need to do it now. She didn't say this to him.

Unable to hide his disappointment at her stark change of mood from the previous evening, Robert said, "Whenever you're ready, I'll drive you up there. They stay open on Sundays for registration."

During the short drive, neither knew what to say, so they didn't say anything. On arriving at the building, Madeline said she could manage the rest on her own. Robert pulled the duffel from the back seat of the car and handed it to her, looking bewildered. Madeline thanked him for everything he'd done for her.

After registering, Madeline, her bag over her shoulder, approached the dormitory to which she'd been assigned in graduate student housing. The bright orange, brick dormitory had the shape of an enormous box of Saltines lying on its side, with two rows of sharp-edged rectangles punched into it.

As she climbed the stairs to the second floor in the dank stairwell, Madeline felt something inside her collapsing. The straight, windowless second-floor corridor was punctuated by nondescript white doors on both sides. As she walked the hallway to her room, she noticed that some of the doors had been painted with a thick, white enamel paint through which she could discern, when the angle of the hallway lighting was just right, the remnants of obscene drawings, and words that had been cut into these doors. Though Shields Hall was now a women's graduate student dormitory, the cuts could only mean it had once been a men's dormitory. She didn't know men well enough to understand what this was all about. Madeline tried to imagine what it would feel like to take pleasure in making these crude carvings, but found she couldn't. She felt more confused than she felt disapproving. It was as if she'd lived in a static world during the years she cared for her mother. One day was the same as the next. Nothing seemed to change. She'd had virtually no contact with boys and men her age other than rushed conversations after class, which seemed to evaporate leaving nothing in their trail. She was an embittered innocent and had no wish to be either embittered or innocent.

Madeline used the key she'd been given at the registration desk to open the door to Room 232.

ELEVEN

Alone in her dormitory room the following morning, Madeline passed by the oval mirror held in a stainless steel stand on the dresser—one of several things she found in the room that had been left behind by the previous occupant. A fleeting fragment of an image in the mirror caught her eye. It was an image of herself as a little girl, watching her mother at her dressing table as she applied soft, astonishingly red lipstick with a lithe movement of her hand, then pressed her lips together as if they were kissing one another. And then there was that pitch-black pencil that she applied to the deepest layer of her upper and lower eyelids, making a line that transformed the mundane into what seemed most delicately and most powerfully female. She rubbed rouge on both cheeks, spreading it with lovely pirouettes of her hand, leaving just the slightest rose color that seemed to glow from within her. And then the ceremony of the earrings: inserting the spoke at the back of her diamond earrings into the hole in each of her earlobes, and, finally, holding her hair aside as she looked at the earring reflected in the mirror, first one side and then the other. She had so wished to grow up and be exactly like her mother.

Gently turning the mirror to its reverse side, Madeline found an image of her face so large that it startled her. What she saw was not a face but a collection of parts, as if it were a slide being viewed through a microscope for medical purposes. Madeline almost never focused her eyes on her face when looking in a mirror. Her father had told her she was very pretty when she was a girl. She believed he thought she was pretty, but maybe that was just because he loved her. Later, when boys looked at her, she didn't know how to respond.

She wasn't only a pretty little girl to her father. She was that and also more than that. He loved to teach her "boy things," such as how to rake leaves in the fall and pull crabgrass in the summer, but she was always a girl for him. She remembered every Saturday morning washing the car with her father, even in the winter when the soapy water in the gray metal bucket was freezing cold; she would sit next to him in the newly washed car as they talked while driving to the hardware store to buy square pieces of wire mesh to repair the holes in the screens in the summer, and the eye-hooks they needed for the gate in the backyard, and a screwdriver that was like a Russian doll with smaller and smaller screwdrivers inside of it until you got to the tiniest one, the baby of the family—though she never said that last part out loud because that would be too girlish a thing to say in a hardware store.

Madeline awoke from these memories to find herself still standing in front of the mirror, feeling nostalgic for those times with her father, and at the same time, feeling the searing pain she'd felt when, in speaking just a few words, he had changed the world: "Sweetheart, I'm not going to be living here with you and Mommy while she and I iron out a few things." Those were his precise words, which she could still hear him speaking— cowardly words with which he'd lied to her, for she knew even as he was saying them that she would never again live in the same house with him, never again wash the car with him or go to the hardware store with him. That part of her life was over, and she knew it before he finished speaking that sentence.

But there she was standing in front of the bureau looking at this curious instrument called a mirror in which only once in a great while had she summoned the courage to look at herself, to really look at her face instead of looking at it in an unfocused way. She must have hoped that Madeline would look different from Carol. That seemed like a stretch, but it was possible. She had to admit that she hoped she looked good, or at least all right. But why was she bothering? What difference did it make? But that was the whole point—it *did* make a difference, and *that* was what was different. It was embarrassing to think that she wanted to look pretty to Robert. She had often been told how pretty she was, but Madeline felt she didn't really know what the word *pretty* meant. It was difficult for her to admit to herself that that's what she wanted to be. How would she know if the face she saw in the mirror was a pretty face? Her mother had been beautiful, but wishing to look like her mother was now impossibly complicated. She'd attended high school, but she'd never really been *in* high school. She'd attended college, but as a townie. She'd never missed living the life of a high school girl or a college girl, until now. You learn things like this in high school and college. You can't skip these periods of life and expect to have grown up.

She glanced in the mirror for a fraction of a second, but aborted the glance because she found that she was looking at the magnifying mirror, which didn't interest her; in fact, it repelled her. Madeline flipped the mirror around and forced herself to fix her gaze on the image she saw in front of her. What she saw was the face of someone vaguely familiar. The face in the mirror was looking at her as questioningly, as disbelievingly as she was looking at it. She realized she was looking into the eyes of a person—a young girl, a teenage girl, a grown-up woman, all at the same time—that were not just reflected there, but were looking back at her. She did not move her eyes from those in the mirror, as if they were in a staring contest trying not to be the first to look away. She wasn't looking at the eyes as a whole or even the whole of the irises; she was looking only at the pupils, trying to see the person living in there.

The pupils were black, neither pretty nor ugly, neither inviting nor threatening. It was she, not the image in the mirror, who first broke eye contact—not out of fear, but out of a desire to step back, to look at the face as a whole.

Madeline had the impulse to turn and walk away, as was her wont when confronted by mirrors—the mirror above the sink in her own bathroom, mirrors in public lavatories, reflections in a glass storefront, even her shadow on the sidewalk—but this time she was intent on becoming familiar with, at ease with, the girl-woman she saw in the mirror, who now felt like a shy companion from whom she would never be separated. She and the girl-woman might as well make the best of it, she thought.

Madeline, as she spent time with her companion in the mirror, began to feel that what the two girl-women held in common was profound sadness about having been orphaned by parents they had adored. They both held on to their grudges long past a time when they were of any real value, but the grudges had the imaginary value of holding on to what might have happened or could have happened, which was so much better than what did happen.

TWELVE

A s Madeline walked down the road from the loading docks and steam-spewing aluminum stacks at the south entrance to the campus, she was talking to herself, oblivious to passing cars and to the dried-out oversized maple leaves on the worn, buckled road. Her head was swimming: the chance encounter with a gas station attendant, her asking directions to a blood bank, baptizing herself with a new name, the time-warp diner, the strange house behind the gas station with its walls covered with paintings and its floors with strange sculptures—or was it just amateurish junk?—the filthy windows of the gas station office, the look in his eyes, his concern for her; no name seemed right for him.

When she said his name to herself, it sounded like the name of a man, not a boy—a fully grown man, like her father, not like the names of boys who had asked her out in high school and college. He was a very handsome man with his JFK-like, tousled blond hair and his winning smile, which he didn't dole out indiscriminately. She didn't feel she was part of the physical world of men or that of women. Her own female genitals felt as foreign to her as a man's genitals. She'd seen her father's penis once when he walked out of the bathroom not expecting she'd be there. His penis made sense, somehow, more sense than her own genitals. Her father's genitals were clean.

She remembered her drunken mother splayed out on the living room couch like a large dead, rotting animal. She could feel that sensation in her hands as she tugged down the upper edge of her mother's white nylon panties. Carol recalled how she would turn her head away so as not to have to look at the loose white skin of her mother's buttocks. But she couldn't prevent her mouth—she breathed through her mouth to minimize smelling the odor—from being filled with the rancid air. She could feel the edge of her hand brushing up against her mother's matted pubic hair, against the granular streaks of shit on the cheeks of her ass, and against her mother's vaginal lips, which felt to her like suction cups of a gigantic octopus pulling her into its interior.

From the time she was in eleventh grade, when her father moved out, she'd been the one responsible for "the care of her mother," a euphemism for removing her mother's stinking panties, bathing with a washcloth her mother's ass and genitals, and then, with all her might, dragging her mother to a sitting position so she could pull one leg at a time into clean panties and a clean nightgown, the only two articles of clothing she wore. "Stop it! I can't stand it anymore," she said out loud to herself, and then immediately, in one violent motion, she turned full circle on the road to see if anyone had been listening to what she'd been thinking (and probably saying out loud) all this time. To her great relief, there was no one in sight.

It was hard to tell how close she was now to the gas station because she'd completely lost track of time and had never walked there from the campus. She was anxious about "dropping in" on Robert at work uninvited, and she wanted to scrub from her mind the thoughts and images of her mother's body that had been coursing through it, so that he wouldn't sense them—smell them?

At the end of the stretch of road ahead, she could make out the concrete surface of the gas station. She practiced in her mind a variety of ways of being casual about "dropping by" or "just taking a stroll" … No, "a walk" was better, but she knew it would be impossible for her to feign informality. She resented the fact that her heart insisted on pounding as she approached the gas station. She had never in her life shown interest in a boy or a man, except for her father when she was a young girl, and that was different. Seemingly out of nowhere, she heard a voice calling out, "Madeline!" For a moment, she could neither place the person whose voice she was hearing nor the person named Madeline. The voice calling that name was a kind, welcoming voice. As she located herself, the thought crossed her mind that as foreign as the name Madeline seemed, the word Carol was now just a sound, not a name, and certainly not her name.

A bit stunned, she was very pleased that Robert took the lead in doing whatever it was the two of them were doing. His smile was a warm smile that had elements of her father's face glowing with pleasure at seeing his "favorite girl." What was new and unnerving was that this was the smile of a man, a grown man, genuinely happy to see her—not as his favorite girl, but as a grown woman whom he liked very much.

"Madeline, I've been hoping you'd come visit after you got your footing up there."

"Of course I'd come for a visit," she replied with warmth in her voice that surprised her. As she heard herself say, "How've you been?" a look of chagrin crossed her face and she turned red with embarrassment, chastising herself for the banality of the question.

"How've I been? I've been hoping to see you again is how I've been. I couldn't very well come knocking on the door of a women's dorm. They still keep the front door of women's dorms locked, don't they? They used to have a kind of reception person on duty at the locked front door. But that's way before your time … I'm blithering."

Madeline smiled softly. She felt calmed by the sound of his voice, and genuinely surprised that he was happy to see her.

"It's windy out here. Let's go into the office."

"I don't want to get in your way during a work day."

"That's a big part of what I like about this place. The four of us are fully at ease with one another. We're fine with whatever it is any of us wants to do. We cover for one another without even noticing we're doing it."

As they walked, Madeline had a glimpse for the first time of the two open garage bays in which three men, considerably older than Robert, dressed in faded blue jumpsuits, were talking, one standing halfway down what seemed to be steps into a pit under one of the cars. She was struck by how lively this place felt compared to the deserted lot it had been when she was there on a weekend.

In the office, Robert moved the chair from behind the desk so it faced the bench where Madeline had napped. He offered her some tea, which again seemed out of keeping with a gas station. She noticed a hot plate with some mugs next to it.

"It's funny," he said, "it feels like a long time ago we were getting you registered and all."

"I appreciate what you did for me. It was very nice … very generous of you."

"I enjoyed it … I was thinking, you and I, we're a lot alike."

"How so?" she said, very pleased to be seen as someone who was not insane.

"Just that you seem surprising, out of the ordinary, which is like me—a guy who works at this gas station, lives in a weird house behind it, paints watercolors, and makes sculptures from junk at night."

"I'd like to think I'm like that, but I'm not. I don't work, I live in a dorm, I don't do anything creative."

"You're studying, reading, writing."

"Mostly I try to get by." She regretted presenting herself in such somber tones.

They sat there in a strained silence. In full morning sunlight, the office looked even dingier than Madeline remembered.

There was a coating of greasy dust on every surface, including the wooden ledge on which her arm was now resting.

"You must be busy, so I won't take up a lot of your time. I just thought I'd say hello and thanks." She stood and turned to see if she'd left anything on the bench.

As she took a step toward the door, Robert blurted out, "I hope you'll drop by again—if you have time, that is?"

"You're sure I won't be in the way?" she said, not liking the words she heard herself saying—too coquettish, she worried.

"No, you're welcome any time. I mean it."

"I've got to get back to campus, so … see you."

Did I really say, "See you," she said to herself.

It was a relief to trudge up the steep incline back to the campus, free of the obligation to act like a normal twenty-two-year-old woman.

THIRTEEN

In mid-October, a powerful wind came up each night that blew in gusts like pounding ocean water that stripped the trees naked, reducing their branches to black lines etched into the mottled gray canvas of the sky. As the road began to be coated with decaying vegetation, the walk to the gas station became increasingly treacherous. One morning after a rain, Madeline found herself halfway down the hill, having fallen a number of times. It would be dangerous to continue down the hill, but it felt impossible to climb back up the road. Each time she began to fall, she could feel the ball of her forward foot losing hold of the ground and her leg suddenly lurching forward, which would propel the rest of her body into freefall. She observed it happening as if from outside herself. The moment when she collided with the pavement, everything stopped: a moment of absolute silence and stillness before she would experience a sharp pain that ran through her arm and hip. As she gathered herself on the ground, she'd move the parts of her arm and torso on which she'd fallen to see if she had sprained something. She'd then push herself to her feet, check for tears in her pants and jacket, brush off the wet leaves, pine needles, and mud, and continue her trek down the hill.

This particular morning, she had reached her limit. She was furious.

When Madeline stepped onto the tarmac of the gas station, her pants soaked through, she met Robert's eyes with a glare of an intensity and severity he'd never seen before in anyone's eyes.

Robert wilted in the heat of her anger. He was well aware that while he had driven her back to the campus most of the time, he had left to Madeline the task of getting herself to the gas station. In the afternoons, she was often given a ride down the hill by an ROTC cadet from a neighboring college or a trucker who'd made a delivery.

Robert walked hastily to the edge of the road where Madeline had planted herself. "You must be freezing," he said, not daring to put his arm around her shoulder to usher her to the office.

"No, I enjoyed the swim down here."

"Come and warm up in the office. The heater's been on for a few hours."

"I'm glad to hear that," she said, her hands reaching deeply into the pockets of her olive-green quilted jacket.

"Let me drive you back to campus so you can change your clothes."

"No, I'll be fine," she said, her eyes averted. She was angrier than she was chilled, but she knew that she had to control her rage if she intended to continue to see this man.

"Please, Madeline, come with me to the office. I'll make you some tea."

Once in the office, Robert boiled some water in a pot on the hot-plate on a rickety wooden table, while Madeline huddled up close to the orange-red bars of the electric heater that had a fan breathing warm air in her direction. With a mug of tea in her hand, Madeline now felt more hurt than angry by the way Robert was treating her.

The visit was unsatisfying for both of them. It was evident that Robert felt guilty about having failed to offer to pick her up, for reasons Madeline couldn't understand—it was so unlike him. Madeline wanted badly to patch things up, but couldn't get herself to say the forgiving words she was trying out in her mind.

On driving Madeline back to campus, Robert offered to pick her up whenever she wanted a lift. Madeline was so upset by what had happened that she didn't think to ask the specifics of how this was to occur.

Two days later, Madeline sat on her bed looking at the black touchpad phone sitting on the table by the bed. It just seemed pathetic. A high-pitched woman's voice was yelling in her head, "No one wants you, so don't go begging!" She hoped that the trembling running through her body wouldn't make her voice quaver.

The phone rang a dozen or so times before Robert picked it up. She'd decided to speak in a breezy tone, as if she were calling on a whim. Robert, on hearing her voice, immediately asked where he should meet her and then answered his own question, saying, "I'll leave now and meet you in the parking area across from the loading docks." He sounded frightened and solicitous; she didn't like that. Calls on days that followed were not quite as unpleasant as this first one, but before making each one, the voice in her head called her demeaning names.

Madeline liked Robert, but she was also very fond of the encapsulated world of the gas station. On days succeeding her explosion of rage, after the drive from the campus to the gas station, they would talk for a while in the office and then Robert would either do some bookkeeping at the desk or go out and tend to something. Madeline would sometimes do her academic work at the desk, but when the sun was bright enough to turn the pewter sky a shiny white-silver, she preferred to sit in the sunlight that bathed the bench under the large front window. With her books and papers spread out before her, she sat twisted to her right on the bench. On days when she felt particularly good, she would sit on the floor with her legs folded under her as she read and wrote.

As one week gave way to the next, it became unnecessary for Madeline to call Robert to ask for a ride. Instead, when Robert dropped her off at the edge of the campus, they would arrange a time for him to pick her up the following day or the day after that, depending on her schedule at the university and his trips to pick up auto parts. She didn't discuss with him the specifics of the way she spent her time: the classes she was taking, tutorials, departmental meetings, teaching assistant obligations, paper deadlines, upcoming exams, and studying in her carrel in the bowels of the library. Robert made it clear, without ever saying so, that he did not want to go any farther into the campus than the parking lot at the south entrance, and Madeline, sensing that it was a delicate matter, never questioned Robert about it. This was one of the deepest forms of care they showed one another—never asking the other to say more than was volunteered.

During the first weeks when Madeline spent time at the gas station, she largely confined herself to the office where she read and prepared for the small groups she taught as a TA—groups of about twenty students, into which large undergraduate lecture courses were divided for discussion. At the gas station office, virtually all the customers were curious about this very attractive girl who seemed to camp out there in the office. Some of the customers tried to strike up conversations with her, as if they were passengers on a long train or airplane trip and happened to be seated next to her. The men certainly noticed her, but usually just stared at her out of the corner of their eye. A few men tried to flirt with her, but her withering look was enough to shut them down. Some of the women her mother's age, and men even older than her father, made comments as if to no one in particular about the early frost, the magnificent fall colors now past, or the three-car accident on Route 12. It seemed to Madeline, but she couldn't be sure, that the women all suspected a romance between her and Robert, but to their credit they kept their thoughts to themselves.

Madeline liked watching and listening as Robert dealt with the customers, largely explaining the work listed on estimates and bills, the breakdown of parts and labor, whether the parts were new or used, and the like. She was struck by the ease and genuine respect with which Robert talked with the customers, many of whom were working-class people for whom the cost of the repairs was a very important matter. Robert spoke to a man a little younger than himself in a way that sounded very much like a kind older brother talking with his younger brother. With men his own age, Robert's voice conveyed the pleasure and genuine camaraderie he felt in talking about sports or local politics; with youngish women, he was friendly and looked pleased to see them, but he did not flirt; with elderly women, he was the good adult son who was glad to see them and could be relied on to protect their interests in the thoroughly male domain of car repair. What was common to the ways he had of being with all of his customers was that he talked in a way that felt to Madeline genuinely personal to each of them.

When Madeline and Robert had time to themselves during the hours she spent at the gas station, they would take a walk, or when it was raining, sleeting, or snowing, they'd stand outside, bundled in their quilted jackets, under the overhang of the roof at the side of the office not far from the door to the restroom. If someone were to have asked Madeline what she and Robert had talked about on any given day, she would have found it very difficult to say, because it really didn't matter what they talked about. What mattered was what it felt like being with him, which she didn't have words to describe. They were curious about each other, but "the facts" about their lives—where they grew up, what their families were like—came out slowly and diffidently. For both of them, the past was so filled with sadness that they hoped it would disappear, or at least let them be, while they tried to get on with their lives.

When they felt there was no way to escape from answering a seemingly harmless question like, "Do you have any brothers or sisters?" they lied, usually by omission but sometimes by lying outright. These unspoken and unanswered questions concerning the lives they'd lived felt far less important to Madeline than how she felt while with Robert, how she felt about him, and how it seemed he felt about her. There was no question that he was a man, not a boy, which helped make her feel like a woman, not a girl, when she was with him.

In the absence of customers, Madeline and Robert were absorbed in their own work, with the comforting background sounds of the clanking of hammer against metal, the high-pitched scream of electric lug bolt fasteners, the occasional hoarse call of one mechanic to another, and now and again a sharp snort followed by the guttural chug of a big rig being downshifted as it gathered strength to make its way up the steepest part of the road to the campus.

By means of ceremonies of hide-and-seek glances between the two—as much as by means of spoken conversation—they began to get to know one another, even to begin to trust one another, though for Madeline, prudence cautioned her not to allow trust to become longing.

After much rehearsal in her mind and many postpone-ments, Madeline said to Robert, "You don't suppose, do you, that I might try talking with the customers, maybe go over a bill or an estimate or something else with them? But please don't worry about offending me if this idea is, for any reason, ridiculous."

Though taken by surprise, Robert, without a moment's hesitation, said, "Of course … If you'd like to try your hand at it, I'd be very happy to teach you. To tell you the truth, I'd imagined that what happens in this place would feel flat and uninteresting to you."

"I'm sorry I gave you that impression. It would mean a lot to me if you'd teach me how to deal with the customers. There was a time I knew how to talk to people. I actually liked it, but I've lost that skill."

Robert smiled as he said, "Hold on, hold on, don't try to talk me out of it."

He stood and pulled the wooden chair in front of the desk to a position next to his chair behind the desk. They sat there, bent forward, shoulder to shoulder, as Robert patiently went over one of the invoices on his desk. Robert's handwriting was striking to Madeline. He printed in a way that reminded her of a Japanese man she'd once seen writing on the sidewalk with a long brush he dipped in water that he carried in a coffee can; he was writing an ancient poem in Japanese calligraphy. The earlier kanji evaporated as he drew the succeeding ones. While thinking about that man, she realized she had completely forgotten that Robert is an artist.

Madeline had difficulty focusing on what Robert was saying as he went over a bill with her. He was explaining the itemization of parts and labor for a car in which a problem with the alternator led to the battery going dead. What he was saying was not conceptually difficult, but she couldn't concentrate on it. The music of the way he was talking reminded her of her father helping her with her homework when she was in junior high school. She cherished those evenings and sometimes pretended not to understand in order to get him to spend more time with her. Those were some of the best parts of her childhood.

"In this portion of the bill, I've listed the repairs that were done, the cost of each of the new and used parts, and the cost of labor …" He continued to explain the invoice, but Madeline couldn't focus her attention sufficiently to follow what he was saying.

Robert, sensing Madeline's withdrawal as he was talking, asked her what was wrong. She told him, "I'm afraid I've put you in a terrible position, asking you to involve me in your work and your life here in this way. I really don't know the first thing about any of it."

Robert moved his chair closer to Madeline's, and she reflexively pushed hers further from his. He said, "Customers don't care about the explanations of the sort I've just given you. Most of them, particularly the women, but all of the customers really, would be grateful to be spared that automotive gibberish. What they do care about is being treated like people, not like customers. They want you to get to know them, to remember when a grandchild's been born or a husband has been ill, which is far more important than the price of a used alternator."

Like a medical student following an intern on rounds, Madeline would stand by the side of the desk as inconspicuously as she could, while Robert, standing in front of the desk—he never sat behind the desk when talking to a customer—explained the different parts of the bill, if the customer wanted an explanation, which they rarely did. What they wanted was talk of different sorts with Robert. Madeline was surprised and touched by the fact that Robert introduced her to customers and told them that she would be helping him in the office. There was no mistaking that the male customers initially felt they'd rather have it the way it had always been, but Robert nipped that feeling in the bud by talking with them in his usual considerate way, and by the time they left they seemed reassured they wouldn't be losing him.

The women customers varied in their response to Madeline's new role according to their age. The older women generally were warm and welcoming to her, as if visiting their daughter at her first job. Some of the younger women, even into their forties, acted as if one of their pleasures in life, flirting with Robert, had been taken from them, and they were not supposed to notice—and to make matters worse, they were expected to help the younger, prettier girlfriend feel at home here.

For Madeline, a disturbing part of being introduced to the customers as Robert's assistant were the memories that came to her of the time she'd spent with her father taking care of "their car"; it had felt like their car, not the family car and certainly not her parents' car. Images came at her like hailstones, memories of her father lifting the thick sponge slobbering with foam as he pulled it from the bucket of cold soapy water, showing her how to unscrew the red glass taillight, lifting her so she could put her full weight on one of the bars of the lug wrench as they replaced a flat tire with the spare. Not only the images, but the words, the names, the sensations, were once precious to her, but now they mostly carried the sting of betrayal.

Madeline found that talking with the customers as Robert's assistant radically changed who she was to the customers and who they were to her, and even who she was to herself. What most astonished her was that when she talked with customers, conversation seemed to come naturally to her. She had become acquainted with some of the customers when she'd been "just reading" on the bench in the office or sitting on the floor, but now she was getting to know them in a way that felt different to her. She found she could remember what they'd talked about the previous time they'd been in, which was an ability new to her. She learned when to be methodical and organized, and when to be ditsy in a comical, self-effacing way, and when to be as bewildered as the customer by the cost of a part, and to check with Robert to see if there was an error concerning the price, even when she was quite sure there wasn't. All the different ways she talked with customers worked because she actually liked almost all of them.

Mrs. Baxter was the first customer Madeline came to know in a way that felt genuinely personal. She was a petite woman, in her seventies, Madeline thought, with the most striking blue eyes—luminescent—and she found something of interest in everything her gaze fell upon. "My husband died years ago and I wouldn't want to trouble anyone by asking them to do all the driving it would take to drop me off and pick me up here. Women my age are afraid to drive—too many things to keep track of at the same time. Anyway, what better thing do I have to do than sit here in this warm room with you? And now I have the pleasure of talking with you for a few minutes, but I don't want to take you away from your reading."

"No, you're not interrupting," Madeline said, as she repositioned herself on the bench to face Mrs. Baxter, who was sitting on one of the two straight-backed wooden chairs, shifting her body to try to find a more comfortable position.

"If this is the first year you're here—or maybe that doesn't matter—this is a wonderful place to live. The marsh, which has been here for centuries, draws so many beautiful birds: the chickadees, white-crowned sparrows, black-throated loons. You can hear them singing to one another the whole of the spring and summer. They're amazing, beautiful creatures. And they're tough, flying a thousand miles south for the winter. And some brave the winter here so you can hear them sing every morning even on the coldest days. Let yourself listen to the birdsong. You'll be hearing something most people don't hear because they're only listening to their own thoughts or to the news on their radio. Well, I'm jabbering like an old lady, so I'll let you get back to your reading."

"I'm an odd duck, better at listening than talking, but not all that good at either," Madeline said, pleased about the unplanned pun, but surprised by having been truthful in what she'd said about herself.

"Well, it's good to be odd, I think. At least it has been for me. If you're afraid of being odd, you aspire to being normal, and being normal, so far as I can tell, is a dull way to be."

After pausing briefly, she continued, "I've seen you there on the bench in the sunlight, and you seem to be all wrapped up in what you're reading, a good reader like my husband was. He was a very good man. I guess that's why I trust men. Don't say this to Robert, but I don't think men are as smart as women. They know how to do things—change fuses, fix cars, unclog sinks—but women know what's actually going on. Men are clueless; they're like little boys, which I find charming." Madeline thought the way Mrs. Baxter spoke was beautiful.

"Mrs. Baxter …"

"Robert is very formal about calling me Mrs. Baxter but no one else is, so please call me Kate."

"Kate's a lovely name."

"Madeline's one of my favorite names. If I were to have a daughter now … which would be quite a thing at my age … I'd name her Madeline. I'm sure you know the French children's story of Madeline."

"Yes, I love that story about the little French girls who 'walked in two straight lines.' My parents weren't readers and didn't read stories to me." This was half true. Her parents didn't read very much, but her mother had read *Madeline* to her many times. Madeline didn't know why she'd lied to Mrs. Baxter.

Some days later, Mrs. Baxter arrived at the office in a winter coat that made her appear to be living in a cave she carried around. She said she wanted to see if her car needed more antifreeze now that the nights were so cold, but her story was so clearly a fabrication that Madeline couldn't suppress a smile. Still wearing her coat, Mrs. Baxter busily tried to settle into the same wooden chair, as much as anyone could settle into such a stern thing, which looked as if it would be more at home in a Calvinist seminary.

As if she were in the middle of a conversation with Madeline, Mrs. Baxter said, "My teenage granddaughter, Lucy, lives with me because her parents have divorced. She doesn't like either of them very much, particularly her mother, my daughter. Lucy is a firecracker—she's seventeen going on twenty-seven. We talk together at dinner and while we clean up afterwards. Last night, we were talking about movies; she loves movies, especially foreign films. I like some of them. She lets me go with her when they're showing here at the university. Some of them are quite sexually explicit. You know what she said to me last night, she said, 'Gramma, our generation is different from yours. We have sex, we have lots of sex, we have sex *all the time*.' I said to her, 'Lucy, you may not believe this but, when I was a girl, we had sex, a lot of sex, we had sex all the time, too, but we didn't always use our whole bodies to do it.' Lucy rolled her eyes, which I found so dear and so funny. I had to suppress a laugh."

Madeline felt as if she'd been talking with her grandmother, the one who had died when she was eight.

FOURTEEN

Robert met Madeline at the south entrance to the campus just before dawn. The rain, which had begun the previous evening, was now only a gauzy haze. Not yet fully awake, the two made awkward comments about the rain during the short drive to the gas station.

Robert parked in front of the office.

"You didn't think I was going to let you go out without breakfast, did you?" Robert said in a tone that sounded to Madeline like a poor parody of a mother. She hoped it was a parody.

The slate pathway to the house was under an inch of water, unlit except for the light over the restroom door at the side of the office. On taking her first step into the house, Madeline was struck, as if awoken by sharp cold water, by the difference between what she was seeing and what she recalled.

This time, stepping into the room, her attention was drawn to a large painting on canvas directly in front of her, a painting devoid of perspective: it depicted three flat, whitewashed rectangular houses with red sloping roofs; the houses stood at the edge of a green-black sea that seemed to be moving. The moon, not far above the horizon, was a circle of reddish orange with an under-layer of sunflower yellow; and from behind the chimneys of the houses, dominating the action of the painting, golden orange, swirling in vine-like spirals which rose gracefully all the way to the top of the canvas and beyond.

"That painting of the houses and the sea and the sky is your painting, you painted it?"

"Yes, I did."

"It's wonderful. Was it here when I first came to your house?"

"In exactly the same place."

"It's … I don't have words for it."

Robert was stunned as much by the softness and tenderness in Madeline's voice as by the words she spoke.

"It's one of my favorites," he said.

Madeline's gaze was pulled farther into the cave-like room, lit only by the overhead lights and table lamps since the windows were still almost black. The walls were covered with paintings and drawings of a variety of sizes and shapes, some on canvas, some torn from a drawing pad, others on what looked like ordinary white typing paper. The abundance felt to Madeline like a classroom of children, each with their hand raised excitedly, eagerly asking to be recognized. Madeline, feeling that she'd never been in this room before, walked from one wall to the next.

She knew that in allowing her into his house this second time, Robert was entrusting to her something private.

Madeline lifted her gaze to take in the sprawling room in which she was standing. The house felt entirely different to her this time: a single room, a kitchen to the left, to the right what might at one time have been a living room, but was now a space dominated by a work table. The table held paint brushes thick and thin, glasses of murky purplish water, and beyond it, pushed up against the far wall with its arms piled high with books, was the couch she'd slept on. It didn't look like the same couch, but Robert wouldn't have replaced that one with another one.

Madeline noticed on the floor, just before she stepped on them, a group of pastel drawings that exuded colors lush and rich and sensual.

At some point—she didn't know how long she'd been looking down at the pastel chalk drawings—Robert said, "There's years of work here and I can't get myself to take down old stuff, so I just make new places for the new things."

The kitchen to the left was an uncluttered place, peaceful and orderly, at the center of which was a dark wooden table, which Robert had set for two.

When Robert dropped Madeline off at the campus the previous day, he said he'd have to be up at 5:30 the next morning to get to "the junkyards." "Otto's been waiting a couple of days now for a piece he needs to complete a repair. Visiting the junkyards can be interesting. I don't suppose you'd like to come with me."

"You suppose wrong." It was evident to Madeline that Robert would very much like her to see this other world. She could tell he took pride in being the only one of the group of four men at the service station who knew how to speak the language of the mechanics and the language of the people at the junkyards.

When they left the house, Madeline walked at Robert's side to the row of cars on the lot. He'd chosen the TR3 for the outing, which stood in line like a battered, war-weary soldier, its paint a dull white that had a faint shine to it because of the thin coat of water it wore from last night's rain. Its canvas top was torn in places, and its plastic rear window had devolved into an opaque dirty gray. Robert opened the passenger door for Madeline as he told her about his fondness for this car while she looked skeptically at its torn leather seats and the original, rubber-coated cord that served as a door handle.

He said they could take the Buick or the old Cadillac if she preferred. Madeline felt as if she were being asked if she wanted to take a favorite toy rifle away from a ten-year-old boy.

As Robert pulled out onto to the road, it was evident he was in high spirits, talking far more than Madeline had ever heard him talk. He told her Otto had asked him to try to find a used generator for a 1965 Austin-Healey. The pre-dawn mist made it impossible to see more than fifteen feet in any direction. The occasional truck coming from the opposite direction made its presence known first by the high-pitched whine of the engine, followed almost immediately by the sight of a blurred mass hurtling itself at them out of the gray mist, and an instant later a thick sheet of water pounded the car. Water began to drip through the holes in the canvas top and siding. Madeline's body tensed as Robert drove the almost invisible road. He didn't slow the car; in fact, he speeded up as he drove through the water pooled in the troughs of the road and seemed to enjoy the thump of the water as it hit the underside of the car. Madeline was not amused, but said nothing.

As the sky ahead took on a pale yellow color at the horizon, the mist enveloping the car dissolved, revealing flat fields on both sides of the road, spotted with stark, leafless trees and strips of decrepit barbed-wire fences. Every now and again they passed a small house huddled up to the side of the road with handwritten signs reading EGGS or APPLES or FIRE-WORKS painted in black on a short piece of shingle attached to a stalk of wood. The signs were so weathered that it seemed unlikely they still meant what they said.

As they approached a town, a metal sign proudly announced its name, along with its population. The town itself was a row of single-story buildings in various degrees of decay. Only one brick building—a bank—sat between a feed store and a general store. The stores were dark at this hour. Three men, their hair soaked, not bothering with hats, coats, or umbrellas, stood at a street corner, holding brown bags out of which the tops of liquor bottles peeked. Three drunkards on a street corner waiting for nothing. The place looked like the setting for a black-and-white film of 1930s rural American desolation.

Madeline was pulled from her half-sleep as Robert turned into a narrow, badly paved road that plunged into thick woods of deciduous trees that looked like the remains of a forest fire. Prickly-looking bushes climbed ten feet or so to the lowest branches of the lifeless trees. A wall built of gray-black stones, seemingly without purpose, ran along the side of the road and then turned and disappeared into the brush, only to reappear some distance ahead.

Robert braked suddenly to turn into a parking area of packed dirt that seemed to defy the rain. They parked next to a muscular, dark-red tow truck with a long bed. The parking lot ended at the mouth of an enormous rust-stained, corrugated metal Quonset hut that stretched back into the woods.

Though not yet 7:00, it could have been midday judging by the activity of the men walking briskly in and out of the hut. As they approached the hut, Madeline began to make out an over-sized man in a full-length brown coat, possibly leather, wearing a cowboy hat, seated behind a card table. As she stepped closer, she could see the deeply furrowed skin on his face, the ruts looking like cracks in a desert floor. He was an almost comic figure, king of the junkyard, his throne a folding chair. His long greasy hair fell from under his leather cowboy hat and draped onto the collar of his coat, and a dead cigar hung from his lips.

"Hey, Slim, that purdy girl beside ya's too good for ya'."

"She ain't dumb neither," Robert said hoarsely.

"So what ya lookin' fer here?"

"I'm lookin' fer a used generator for a 3000 Mark III Healey, 1960 or '61."

The man seemed to be giving some thought to it.

"A used generator for a 1960 3000 Mark III Healey," Robert repeated.

"Sonny, I may be old, but I ain't deaf … There ain't much call fer parts fer a fancy car like that 'round here. Buddy'll be in. He'll have a look."

"When's he comin' in?" Robert said, knowing he wasn't going to get anything more out of him. Madeline was amused as she watched this man who pretended to be some sort of hillbilly, but wasn't.

"He jest show up when he do," the seated man said wearily and turned his head as if looking for someone or something, which was the signal to Robert that his audience with "the Duke" was over.

Once she and Robert had moved away, Madeline laughed a genuine laugh. "I can't say I like the man, but I enjoyed the show. I'm sure he gave himself that name."

"We could walk up this road a quarter mile or so while we wait. There's one of those Carvel or Dairy Queen stands up there. Maybe it's open. They might have coffee," Robert said, fearing he was losing her attention with every word he said.

They passed an abandoned stand with a flaking, hand-painted sign that said FIREWORKS. Robert explained, "They're selling cherry bombs—extremely powerful round, pinkish-red things with a green fuse that makes them look like a cherry. Farmers shove them lit into gopher holes, and junior high school kids buy them to blow up something in their backyard. You'll lose your hand if it blows up while you're holding it." Madeline tried to act interested.

The Dairy Queen was closed and they walked up the road a while more until Madeline spotted an empty parking lot with four-foot metal poles sticking up next to each parking place. An enormous white wooden wall folded in on itself stood in front. It took half a minute or so before Madeline realized that THE GOLIATH—the name painted in faded red letters on a sign precariously balanced on the roof of the remains of a shack-like structure—was an abandoned drive-in movie theater.

"I went to a drive-in movie when I was a kid," Madeline said. "They were almost entirely gone by the time I was a teenager.

Our children won't believe that such things actually existed." She immediately regretted having said "our children."

When they returned to the junkyard, the Duke yelled, "Hey, kid, Buddy's back."

"Where is he?"

The Duke ignored the question.

Madeline's attention was glued to a woman in her fifties or sixties whose forearm had been amputated a few inches below the elbow. She was wearing a sleeveless blouse, as if daring anyone to stare at the stump. She'd hooked the black strap of her fake alligator skin handbag in the crook of her elbow. Madeline was terrified by the sight.

Her voice trembling, Madeline said to Robert, "Put your arms around me and hug me as tightly as you can. Go ahead, please. Squeeze as hard as you can. Don't worry that it's too tight. Please do it now. I'll explain later." She never did.

He put his arms around her until his hands clasped one another while pressing against Madeline's back. He'd never before touched her. She was smaller and lighter than he'd expected. He felt like he was holding a shivering bird.

"Squeeze harder, please. Just hold me very, very tight."

She pushed her face into his neck as if burrowing into him. He could feel the warmth of her breath on his neck. Her hair was soft and light on his face.

As she stood there with Robert's arms around her, Madeline could feel a sense of calm run through her body but worried she'd shown him more of herself than she wanted to.

Robert slowly loosened his embrace as he felt the pressure of Madeline's grip on his back begin to ease. Looking in Madeline's direction but not at her face, he said, "Why don't we go back to the university so you can get some rest?"

"Don't be silly. You'd be doing me a favor if you just went on as you usually do when you buy used parts at places like this … I mean it."

As they walked back toward the front of the Quonset hut, the Duke, catching sight of them, said, "Little lady, we don't get much like you round these parts."

Madeline looked him in the eye and said, "Why are you talking like a character out of an old Western?"

The Duke looked up at her and said, "You're a sassy one, ain't ya, missy?"

"Give me a break. Where's Buddy?" she snapped in reply.

He motioned with his head toward the hut.

On stepping further into the windowless, cave-like structure, Robert said sternly, "What was that all about back there? The Duke's not malignant and he's not a fraud. He's a character."

"I don't want to be a character in his play. He's free to be that character, but not with me. You need him; I don't. He knows I have nothing to lose, which makes me scary."

"I don't find you scary."

"You should. I mean it."

Out of the darkness of the cave a man approached them, a lanky man, at least six foot two, wearing a white T-shirt and army-green work pants. His face was ravaged by old acne scars. In a raspy voice, he said without looking at either of them, "Buddy here," and then turned and walked into the tunnel. They followed as if entering a shrine. The Duke must have told him which auto part they were after because Buddy didn't ask.

Robert and Madeline followed into the dank semi-darkness. As they walked deeper into the recess, the industrial lights hanging from the ceiling gave way to jerry-rigged overhead fluorescent lights, connected to one another and to outlets near the floor by lengths of thick red extension cord draped over the metal racks like strings of Christmas tree lights. The fluorescent tubes cast a flickering bluish luminescence over the rows of six-foot-long, gray metal racks, six or eight shelves high.

Robert glanced over at Madeline periodically with a concerned expression on his face, which was met by a glare of resentment for being treated like a child, or worse yet, a weak and vulnerable girl.

Buddy knew exactly where he was going, turning his head neither to the right nor the left. On arriving at the area he'd been seeking, he said to Robert, "Austin 1960 3000 Mark III Healey aftermarket generator. It's a 6-volt, 25-amp, negative lead generator. Got one here. It came in a while ago. Never thought we'd sell it. Told Duke not to buy it, but he bought it anyway 'cause he likes the fella that was sellin' it. Been sittin' here a long time. Mark III, a nice car, engine block's for shit, but nice-lookin'." The fact that Buddy was speaking to Robert in complete sentences was as unexpected to Madeline as hearing a dog speak.

"What's it gonna run?" Robert asked.

"A hundred 'll do it, I think."

"Tell the Duke forty," he said over his shoulder as he walked into the even deeper reaches of the hut.

Robert and Madeline were quiet as they drove back to the gas station. The sky was filled with an enormous storm cloud from which they could see faint vertical lines of rain against the horizontal line of pale gray sky between the clouds and the horizon.

"Now you know a little more about the world I live in," he said.

"And you, unfortunately, know a little more about me."

"Unfortunate for who?—not for me. I like getting to know you."

"I like to keep to myself."

Robert made no reply, as if his attention were fixed on the road.

"You keep to yourself, too," she added.

"What do you mean, I keep to myself?"

"Don't act dumb. You have more secrets than anyone I've ever known, except me."

"What are you talking about?"

"Do you think I'm stupid or blind? The gas station is a make-believe gas station. You don't know that?"

"Know what?"

"It's a money-laundering operation."

"Are you crazy?"

"Yes, I am crazy, but I'm not stupid."

"What's gotten into you, Madeline? The gas station's not a money-laundering operation. You've been reading too many detective novels."

"Pull the car over to the side of the road."

"What's going on?"

"Just do it."

After Robert had turned into a side road and parked the car, Madeline gathered herself before turning to look Robert in the eye. "Are you really blind to the fact that almost everything at the gas station is done in cash; most of the vendors are paid in cash, the wages are paid in cash, the customers are given big discounts if they pay in cash. The boss shows up furtively once a week, talks to no one, goes to the back room of the office, locks the door, does something with whatever's in the locked file cabinets, buys and sells the row of cars that nobody knows about, owns an abandoned house that he lets you live in out of the kindness of his heart—as part of your wages, I guess, or maybe just to make you indebted to him? Is none of that apparent to you?" Her face was red and tears were welling in her eyes.

"Look, Madeline, I don't like having you lecture me as if I'm a moron. You've been around the station for only a few months, a few hours at a time, while I've been there for years …"

"Stop talking. You're just blithering. Think about it."

"I don't want to think about it. You're talking about my home, my friends, and you're turning the whole thing, my whole life, into shit."

Madeline was reminded of how boyish this man had seemed to her when he took her to the diner, a place the two of them go now primarily to say hello to the waitresses. She recalled how he'd beamed when he first took her there and introduced her to the middle-aged women who had taken him under their wing like a lost puppy. He'd been desperately lonely, she now knew, and very naïve for a man twenty-six or twenty-seven years old—he'd never told her exactly how old he was. He was much younger than his chronological age, as she was, but she did have the sense to be cynical—about everything.

They completed the drive back to campus in silence, Robert sulking, and Madeline wanting to apologize but unable to do so. What she'd said had been true, she said to herself, but did she really have to say it?

FIFTEEN

Robert and Madeline had begun to take walks together on Sundays if the air wasn't bitterly cold, if it wasn't raining, or if the snow wasn't too deep—at least one of which happened about half the Sundays of the winter. On this Sunday in December, Robert waited in his car at their usual meeting place at the south entrance. He startled slightly as Madeline pulled open the door on the passenger side. Then—and this was something Madeline deeply appreciated about Robert—his face filled with a look of boyish joy that what was happening was just as he'd hoped it would be. This expression on Robert's face melted the awkwardness Madeline felt as she saw the car with its engine running and white exhaust huddling around the tail pipe. He turned off the engine and they walked to the beginning of the path down the side of the ridge into the valley.

The warmth of the sun that day allowed them to wear woolen sweaters instead of the winter coats and parkas they'd been swaddled in for the previous week of sub-zero temperatures. They set out side by side along the path, their boots pressing down the half-frozen grass on each side of the narrow trail. Madeline found herself taking Robert's hand. It had been at least a decade since she had held anyone's hand—her father's hand when she was ten or twelve. But this was different from holding her father's hand. Holding Robert's hand felt at once odd and right. The sensation of heat in her fingers squeezed between his spread through her.

Only after some time did her mind turn to the feeling of the warmth, or was it heat, of the skin of *his* hand in hers, a body that wasn't hers right up against hers, and she wanted it never to stop being what it was at that moment. But she had no confidence that she wouldn't spoil things, as she so often did. She had never touched or been touched in that way by anyone. She languished in these sensations and felt no wish to focus her eyes on anything. For quite some time it didn't occur to her to look at the man whose hand she'd taken. He would have been an unwanted intruder had he said anything or turned to look at her—and he seemed to know that.

As surprising and odd and right and worrisome as her taking his hand had been, she found herself bringing the movement of her feet to a halt, looking up at him, moving her face so close to his she could feel his warm breath on her face. It felt unexpectedly natural to put her lips on his and to kiss him and to feel her kiss received and returned. That kiss turned into another, and another, both of them growing hungry for more. Then Robert, on his own, without asking permission, without needing permission, parted her lips with his tongue—her teeth seemed to disappear as a part of her body—entered her mouth, and explored that soft warm space. She had read about this in novels, but what she was feeling couldn't be conveyed in words or images. She was painfully aware that twenty-two was a freakishly old age to be experiencing this part of life for the first time. She liked Robert very much, but this kind of kissing was an entirely different thing from liking. She loved the feeling of being ravished, which she would never have anticipated. She at first timidly pressed her tongue against his lips, and when she could wait no longer, entered his mouth, not knowing what she would find or feel. She was astonished by the fact that their mouths ceased being places and became feelings. Beginnings and endings were determined, she found, by the intensity of the passion, which ebbed and flowed, sometimes settling into a restful doze before returning flood-like.

As she remained in his embrace after they stopped kissing, she felt that he wasn't the same person to her now, nor was she the same person she'd been. She felt beautiful for the first time in her life, and felt profoundly grateful to this man, Robert, for making her feel that way. He'd been so patient and waited for her so long.

As they resumed walking, the silence between them was brimming with things felt but not needing to be said.

Eventually, Madeline said, "I think there are at least six senses—the usual five, which we share with most other animals, and then there's the experience of beauty, which I think only humans can feel."

"You are beautiful—*really* beautiful and *really* sexy," he said in a way that only he could say it—serious and sincere, but with an edge of impishness.

As they followed the path along the side of the marsh, a breeze came up that carried the chill of winter, but Madeline was so lost in her thoughts and feelings that she was oblivious to it, aware of almost nothing other than the feeling of her hand in Robert's. The feelings she'd had while kissing him remained in her body in the form of a sense of softness, a rare feeling for her. She wondered if the feelings she was having were what it meant to be normal. She'd always claimed, and believed, that she didn't aspire to being normal; she wanted to be strange, weird, an outsider. But no one asks you if you want to be a weird outsider. It's not a choice you make.

SIXTEEN

Madeline felt as if she had entered another universe as she sat behind the desk in the office of the gas station later that day. Life's problems and pleasures at the gas station were of a different sort, a far simpler sort from the ones she'd wrestled with since she was ten. When a customer raised a question about a bill or an estimate, Madeline would walk to the garage, sheet of paper in hand, feeling all the pride of a grade-school girl chosen by the teacher to take an envelope to the principal's office. When Madeline talked with Charlie, the mechanic Robert felt closest to, about a bill or estimate, she felt businesslike, but also feminine in a way that reminded her of the good years with her father. The other two mechanics, Otto and Joe, were shy but accepting of her, glad that Robert had a girlfriend, the first he'd had during the time they'd known him.

Madeline felt tenderness in the gentlemanly manner with which the mechanics treated her, which helped her to feel dignified after she'd spent so many years of her life feeling squalid.

It was evident to Madeline that the three mechanics, all in their mid- to late fifties, were fond of Robert; they were fathers to him, each in his own way. The gas station's car repair business had grown over the course of the past few years, in part, many of the customers told her, because of the calm and easy way the four men worked with one another and with them. In "bits and pieces," Robert told Madeline something about each of the mechanics, but never betrayed what he felt to be confidences they'd entrusted to one another.

About Charlie, he'd said, "His wife died just before I began working here. I've picked up from the other mechanics that Charlie was quite different before his wife died—a man glad to see you each morning, a guy who liked to listen to music on the radio as he worked, and once in a while sang along with a song that was playing. He and his wife didn't have children, so he's alone now in the apartment where the two of them lived for more than thirty years. He had, and still has, a wicked sense of humor, but he never turns it against his friends. He always gets a laugh from Otto, Joe, and me when, under his breath, he calls the boss 'a wolf in cheap clothing' when the boss walks from his car to the office."

About Joe, he'd said, "He's the diagnostician. I sometimes watch him open the hood of a car, start the car, sit in the driver's seat letting the sounds and vibrations run through him. He then steps out of the car and slowly walks around it, stopping now and then to slide under the car on his back to put his hands on the drive train and exhaust system, and then gets up to complete the circuit, inspecting the body for rust. He takes the car for a test drive, which he insists on doing alone. When he gets back, it's as if he's gotten to know the car intimately, almost as if he's slept with it and has come to know all of its secrets."

And about Otto: "I think Otto's probably the best mechanic of the three. He escaped the Nazis and came over here with his uncle when he was just a kid. I've never asked him about his accent. I think it's Hungarian, but I don't know for sure. I don't think Charlie or Joe do either. I like his accent. He hasn't said a word about his family, and nobody asks. Otto works on the foreign cars, like the Austin-Healey we got a part for."

One day when he and Madeline were alone in the office, Robert said, "I know I haven't told you about the boss.

122

He's a detestable man—shady—he makes me feel dirty just being around him. He doesn't really have a name except on some papers he's signed in illegible writing. We just refer to him as 'the boss.' He's probably a crook. You were right about all the things you said about this place: it's heavily a cash business, far more than usual for a service station like this. The boss doesn't exchange a single word with the mechanics. The cars lined up on the far side of the lot appear and disappear at night. I've seen men get dropped off here to take one of the cars, but they don't say anything to me.

"When the boss comes by every Thursday at closing time, it's as if I'm not even here in the room with him. He picks up the ledger and stack of invoices I keep on the desk, goes to the back room, which he keeps locked, and spends an hour or so in there."

"I'm sorry to have been right, and even sorrier about the way I pummeled you with it," Madeline said. "This place is your home and your family. It's the best family I've ever seen. I see the way the four of you eat your lunch together at the far end of the garage. I make myself scarce during that lunch break, but now and again I catch a glimpse of the four of you sitting there in the corner of the garage with your thermoses at your feet.

"Sometimes when I'm in the office with the windows open, I hear the four of you laughing together, real belly laughs, and it makes me feel good to hear it. Other times I just hear the sound of one of you talking—I can't tell which of you it is or what's being said—but it gives me the feeling that one of you is telling a story and the others are listening carefully."

"I don't know what to say. You describe it much better than I could. You surprise me."

"What's surprising?" she said with sadness in her voice. "You're surprised I can feel things and sense things?"

"No, I know you feel things. Oh, I meant to tell you, I'm just astounded by the way you're able to flesh out with such

123

accuracy what it feels like, what I feel like, when I'm with Charlie, Otto, and Joe. These men convey with just a look in their eye, or the way they sit or pour coffee from their thermoses, such caring about one another, such understanding of one another, and about me. You noticed that from little bits and pieces, and to me that's astounding.

"I haven't told you—the other day Charlie said to me that it would be fine, and he and Otto and Joe said it was fine with them, if you joined us for our lunch break. I told him I thought you had better things to do than hang around bums like us."

"You were right to say what you did. I wouldn't dream of changing one thing about your lunch break."

SEVENTEEN

As winter melted into early spring, it was evident to Madeline from the distant look in Robert's eye, the fatigue in his voice, and the way he thrashed about in his sleep that he was upset about something. She thought she might be the cause of his torment. He might want to be alone while he did his artwork, or maybe he was sick of her and didn't know how to ask her to leave. When she asked him if he was upset with her about something, he said, "No, you're not doing anything wrong. I just go through periods like this. They don't last long."

The joy they felt in being with one another seemed to be dying. They hadn't listened to music together in a long time; he rarely asked her for thoughts about his artwork; and she no longer read him passages from books she loved. At night in bed, as they were drifting off to sleep, he had stopped putting his arm around her, and instead tossed in bed in jagged movements as if wrestling. It must be the sex, she thought. They were occasionally having sex, and Madeline felt grateful to Robert for his patience, but she couldn't say she enjoyed it very much.

Finally, one evening, as they sat silently at the wooden table in the kitchen after a supper Robert had hardly touched, she said, "Robert, you're scaring me. Have you lost interest in me?"

"No," he said, surprised by her question. "No, nothing like that."

"But there is something wrong, isn't there?"

"I promise it has nothing to do with you."

"We're in the same house, but not really living together any longer."

He sat silently, looking down at the plate in front of him.

"You have to tell me what's happening."

Robert said, "I'm embarrassed and ashamed and confused."

"You've been so accepting of me, never judgmental. Let me do the same for you."

He said, "There's a lot I haven't told you."

"Don't worry about what you haven't told me. I promise you I have many more secrets than you do."

"There's a whole part of my life I haven't told you about. I try not to think about it. You've probably noticed that I've said a lot about art and a lot about buying used parts and a lot about the mechanics and the boss, but I haven't said a word about what's happening in the world beyond the borders of this gas station. In my years at the university, the anti-war movement was a big part of my life. It was who I was to myself—one of the leaders of the anti-war movement on campus. It was more important to me than art, or the classes I was taking, or friends. It turned out I was charismatic and I'd never felt so powerful. I was asked to be the leader of the SDS on campus at the end of my freshman year."

"I'm ashamed to admit I don't know what that is. I have had so few dealings with the outside world; I'm ignorant about anything beyond myself and my little world."

"Students for a Democratic Society—an anti-war group with chapters on campuses all across the country.

"Getting back to what happened. Spring of my sophomore year, when I was walking between classes, a man who looked like a gangster approached me. He drew me off the concrete path and led me to the side of a dormitory building. He said the work I was doing here had been so successful that I had caught the attention of the national leadership of SDS and they wanted to talk with me about taking a position in the national organization. I was flattered. He gave me the time and place in Chicago where I'd meet with some of the national SDS leadership. So I drove to Chicago. The address he wrote down was in a rundown part of the city.

"The meeting in Chicago felt strange, almost surreal. There were five men in their thirties and early forties. It wasn't a conversation; it was a grilling. The wanted to know everything about me, but they were particularly interested in where I stood in relation to violence—how I dealt with police.

"I left feeling dirty. I didn't want to have anything to do with them. I felt so stupid that I hadn't seen it coming. A few weeks later—this was the spring of my junior year—as I was leaving my dorm to go to breakfast, two men in suits and ties, FBI men, were suddenly, out of nowhere standing right in front of me. One of them asked if I was Robert Renfro. They wanted to ask me a few questions. I followed them to an empty conference room. The chairs were set up for the interrogation—two seats on one side of the long table, one on the other. They said they were FBI agents. I asked to see their identification. They each pulled from the inside pocket of their jacket an identification card with their photograph on it and a heavy-looking bronze badge that looked real. How would I know if the badges were real or not? They wanted to know about the meeting in Chicago. Where was it held? Who was there? What were the questions they'd asked? Were there other meetings I'd attended? What plans had they told me about? What was the post they were grooming me for? They kept asking the same questions again and again. And I kept telling them that the men I'd met in Chicago hadn't told me anything about their plans or about my role in their plans. They warned me that I was in very serious trouble for taking part in a meeting with the Weather Underground. Weather Underground is an anti-war group that uses violence—bombing government buildings at night, risking killing anyone in the building. The FBI men told me that even if I didn't participate in carrying out potentially violent assaults, my association with them could lead to my arrest for attempting to overthrow the government, and if anyone was killed by the Weather Underground, I would be arrested for felony manslaughter. After about an hour, they stood up, thanked me for my cooperation, and left the room. The whole time they addressed me as 'Sir.'

"About a week later, I found in my mailbox a letter asking me to meet with the dean of students immediately. He told me I would be given credit for the courses I was taking, but I was not to return to class. He said there was a restraining order out on me, so I would be arrested if I set foot on university grounds again. He said he was only the messenger and couldn't tell me the specifics of why this action had been taken. I said I wanted to appeal this decision. He told me that there was no appeal process connected with this type of expulsion. I told him that I would appeal this in the courts. He said I was welcome to do so.

"While I'm telling you the truth about who I am and what I've done, I might as well make it complete. I was lying to you about the professors in the art department giving me studio space and behaving like fathers to me after I was banned from campus. There was no such invitation. I don't know why I embellished the story like that. I think I wanted to give you the feeling that there is something special about me, that I'm not just a dropout gas station attendant."

Madeline sat back in her chair, her gaze directed just above Robert's head. After a silence, she said, "Robert, I don't understand why this feels shameful to you. You were involved in a large, nonviolent organization opposing the Vietnam War, something to feel proud of. You should feel angry, not ashamed, about being expelled for that."

"It's not as simple as that," Robert said. Madeline chose not to ask what he meant.

Madeline felt not an obligation but a sincere desire to meet Robert's honesty with honesty of her own. "I think we're turning a corner in telling one another who we are. We've respected one another's privacy, which was good at the start, but it's stopped us from getting to know one another well. It's time that I tell you some of what I've kept secret from you. I've been vague. As a little girl, I loved my father as much as any little girl loves her father, and I felt I could trust him to make right anything that went wrong. Then he and my mother entered a vicious cycle: I don't know which came first, my father's affair or my mother's alcoholism. It doesn't matter. He left my mother and me, and it was my job to take care of her. She kept all the curtains in the house closed and lay on the couch, and drank until she passed out. I was in high school, but I felt responsible for her. I was afraid she would die if I didn't take care of her. I felt I had somehow caused the divorce. I hated her and her body. I had to clean her body most days, and this went on for five years. I was ashamed that I didn't have a normal mother and a normal family, so I led a secret life without many friends, lying to everyone. Then, finally, when I graduated from college to come here, I was able to tell my father, 'I quit, I resign, take care of her yourself.' I haven't told you this, but she died last October. I blame myself for her death, and at the same time, I feel relieved she's dead. You can't really know me without knowing all these things. She died by choking on her own vomit a few weeks after I left home to come here, which I told my father she'd do. I didn't go to her funeral, which I sometimes feel guilty about and sometimes feel that not going to anything associated with her was what I should have done years earlier. I can still smell the alcohol, urine, and shit that enveloped us as I cleaned her, removed her dirty clothes, and put clean ones on her. Her filth has become part of me. So there it is, the gist of it anyway."

Robert listened. When she finished, he said, "I'm so sorry you had to go through all that."

While she was talking, she hadn't decided whether she'd tell him about the revulsion she felt for her own body. She thought that, in a way, it wasn't necessary. He'd felt the effects of it, even if he didn't have the full story behind it.

PART IV

THE VISITOR

EIGHTEEN

J ust after dawn that morning in mid-April, Robert took one of the larger pickup trucks to buy an engine block at one of the junkyards. He told Madeline he'd try not to wake her when he left. She woke about 7:00 and was looking forward to spending the day working on her master's thesis.

The room she used as her study had been a storage room for art supplies before she moved in. She and Robert cleaned and painted it in the spirit of newlyweds fixing up their first house. It was now a pleasant space with windows on three sides into which sunlight shone through the evergreens and lit the room. The intermittent clanking sounds of the mechanics at work had become so familiar to Madeline that they had become part of the quietude enwrapping her while she studied. This house behind the gas station felt like a home she hadn't had since she was a girl.

Just before noon that day, Madeline was startled by fierce knocking on the front door. On opening the door a crack, she was confronted by the gaunt face of a tall man staring down at her. His hazel eyes were sunken between the bones protruding around them. His teeth were askew, darkly stained. His body stank.

When Madeline, in a state of shock, took a half step backward, he pushed the door open and said, "Please accept my

133

apologies for interrupting your morning," in a voice that was coldly threatening. It was clear to Madeline that this man was insane and homeless. His gray sweatshirt was grease-stained and frayed at the collar and sleeves. His oversized pants were drawn tight by a belt.

"How can I help you?" Madeline said, feeling her throat tightening.

"There's nothing I need help with."

Finally able to gather herself and look more closely at this man's face, she thought she saw a family resemblance to Robert.

She said to him, "Are you Robert's brother?"

"No, Robert's *my* brother."

"He's not here."

"When's he coming back?"

"I'm not sure."

"When?"

"I don't know. He sometimes goes to pick up parts for the cars," Madeline said.

"This is his house."

"Yes."

"What are you doing here?"

"Studying for my classes at the …"

"So what are you doing here?" he repeated.

On the basis of the facial similarity and the way he spoke, Madeline took her chances with an altogether different tack. "Why don't you come in and wait for him," she said with all the equanimity she could muster.

The man seemed to melt. "I could wait outside if you'd like me to," he said, looking over Madeline's shoulder at the room behind her. It seemed to her that he'd never been inside this house.

"My name's Madeline. Would you tell me your name?"

"Would it be okay if I didn't?"

"Of course."

Madeline stepped backward to make room for Robert's brother to come into the house a step or two. "Would you like something to eat or drink?"

"You live here?"

"Yes."

"Our older brother, James, shot himself in the head."

"My God, that's horrible."

"He never told you, did he?"

"No."

"James was six years older than me, and eight years older than Bobby, so he doesn't remember much about him, but I do."

"He must have been in terrible pain."

"That's right, he was, but not before."

"He was different before he shot himself?"

"Yes, he was. He was a good brother to both of us. He protected Bobby and me. We wouldn't have made it without him. You'd have to know him back then."

"What happened to him?"

"I told you. He shot himself in the head."

"No, I meant what happened that drove him to do that?"

"Arthur did."

"Who's Arthur?"

"I never use the word *father*. He doesn't deserve that name."

"What did he do to James?"

"He killed him."

"How did he do that?"

"By taking every cell in his body and injecting it with poison."

"What kind of poison?"

"Hating him. Beating him. He beat James with words and with a strap, but after a while James refused to cry, which infuriated Arthur. That took all the fun out of it for him."

"Did he beat you and Bobby?"

"It's cold in here."

Madeline felt an ache in her muscles as she stood there. Her mouth felt parched. "I'm going to get a glass of water. Can I get you something?"

"No, thanks. I don't want anything."

He stayed where he was, just inside the front door while Madeline went into the kitchen, which was only a few paces from the front door. After filling the glass, her hand trembled as she lifted it, causing her to spill the cold water all over her hand and wrist. She held the glass with both hands and raised it to her lips as she leaned against the side of the sink, her back to Robert's brother. She felt as if she were defusing a bomb. Not wanting to spill the water all over herself, she carefully lowered the glass into the sink.

When she turned from the sink, he startled. He'd been looking to his right into the part of the house that was diagonally crossed by the clothesline from which paintings on paper were attached by clothespins.

"You're sure you don't want anything?" Madeline said, feeling ridiculous for asking him the same question again, and dreading he'd say yes.

"He's a good artist, really good, he's always been," he said, with what sounded like genuine pride.

"You and Robert were good friends growing up, weren't you?"

"We *are* good friends. More than good friends. We're brothers."

"That's a better way of putting it."

"Do you have a sister?"

"No, I don't."

"You know, you're strange," he said.

"I guess I am. You don't get a choice about that."

"I like being alone."

Madeline didn't know how to keep this repartee going.

"My memory's not good," he said. "Shock treatments. I was in the Army, but they wouldn't give me VA benefits, so I had to go cheap at a third-rate hospital when I got shocked."

"I'm sorry," she said, looking him in the eye as he looked away.

"I have to go now."

He turned up one side of his lips slightly while nodding to her at the door as he left, just as Robert smiled. But this man's smile was entirely devoid of warmth.

When the door finally clicked shut, Madeline could barely keep her balance as she slapped aside sheets of paper hanging from the clothesline on her way to the bedroom. She lay face down on the bed, her arms outstretched in front of her, her muscles aching from the tension.

As Madeline lay there, her fear began to turn to rage. First at Robert's brother for terrorizing her, then at Robert for not warning her that he had an insane homeless brother who might appear, and finally at herself for making such a poor choice of a man with whom to live.

As Madeline lay for a time on Robert's bed, her feelings softened. Robert's brother's "Big Bad Wolf" entry was a childish way of introducing himself to the woman his brother was living with—a person who frightened him, who might steal Robert from him. It probably wasn't an accident that he came to the house at a time when Robert was away. He must have known he'd find her by herself in the house, though he seemed not to know what to make of her, not to know what it meant for his brother to be living with a woman.

She turned the visit over and over in her mind, looking at it from one direction and then another. She hated this man for scaring her. She pitied him. At moments she even admired him. Despite his insanity, his homelessness, he hadn't given up on life; he hadn't killed himself. She couldn't know for sure, but she felt that James, though real to Robert's brother, wasn't a real person—he was another name that Robert's brother had for himself, and this made her want to cry.

NINETEEN

Madeline spent the rest of the day in front of her type-writer, her head swirling, unable to write. Finally, after the mechanics had closed the gas station for the night, she heard a car pulling into the space at the side of the office.

As if her hearing were keener than usual, Madeline could hear the grainy tread of Robert's feet on the snow-covered slate leading to the house. She tried not to pounce on him before he had time to say hello and hang up his coat.

As calmly as she could, she said, "Robert, your brother came for a visit today."

Stunned, Robert said, "He did what?"

"He was here, talking to me."

"What happened?"

"He at first tried to frighten me, but he calmed down, and I calmed down a little. I invited him in. There were things he wanted to tell me. I don't know why. Things I think he thought I didn't know about you and your family and should know, like James, your older brother, who he loved, who protected the two of you, who shot himself in the head—I don't know if he's a real person—and about the fact that he was in the Army and had shock treatment that makes it hard for him to remember things, and …"

"Madeline, I'm sorry …"

"One other thing. He didn't want to tell me his name."

"His name is George. I'm sorry I kept him a secret."

"Why did you?"

"I'm not sure," he said. "All I can tell you is that he's the remainder of a life I wanted to leave behind when I met you. He's like a satellite that revolves around me, invisible to everyone but me. I'm the only thing between him and the gutter or between him and the grave. I love him, but it's complicated."

"Robert, I don't know who you are. Only a few days ago, you told me about a secret part of your life you're plagued by, and today your hand is forced into telling me about another part of your life unknown to me. You told me you were an only child. It's as if you've cut yourself into pieces—I don't know how many—and now I know two new pieces. I wish you trusted me more. In an odd way, I feel I can read George better than I can read you. At least he's trying to tell me things that matter to him, while you're lying to me about what matters to you."

"It's not as if I've had an affair I've kept from you. George is my brother who I loved more than anything in the world when we were growing up. He's a person who I take care of because I want to, but I also want a life of my own. I've never been able to find a way to do it."

"I understand that he's sick and can't survive on his own," Madeline said in a composed voice. "I know this sounds terrible, but I want to be the person who comes first in your life, and I know I can't compete with him. I don't want to compete with him. I refuse to compete with him."

"Madeline, I know my word isn't worth much to you now, but I swear to you that you come first to me."

"I don't think you know what you're saying. If a mother—a decent mother—is asked which of her children she'd sacrifice, it's impossible for her to answer the question. You're lying to yourself when you say I come first to you."

"You're right that I could never abandon George. He was an entirely different person before he had his breakdown in high school. Since then he's been like a child. I'll tell you about him if you want me to, but I wouldn't blame you if you never want to hear another word about him."

"Are you capable of talking to me truthfully about him?"

"I'll try to tell you the truth."

"All right."

Once they were seated at opposite ends of the couch, Robert said, "It's a long story. George is two years older than me, and he was a wonderful big brother to me. He was both a brother and a father to me. He was excited by life, and his amazement about just about everything was exhilarating. He was the most important thing in life to me—far more important than my parents. On school days I looked forward all day to spending time with him after school, mostly in his room, which I moved into because I didn't like being alone when I was asleep. I was in love with him. He read everything he could get his hands on at the library and told me about the thing that was most exciting to him that day. I remember how big his eyes got when he was telling me about the fact that our bodies are almost completely made of air; and that when astronauts are able to fly close to the speed of light, time will slow down while the rest of the people in the world grow old and die; and about the Apache Indians, who have no written language, and in World War II could convey orders to other Apaches at the front lines by talking in their language and the Nazis couldn't decode what they were saying. In a way he was possessed, but not by demons, he was possessed by the fact that the real world is filled with astounding things. And he filled my life with astounding things.

"He and our father did not get along—that's an understatement. I've never been able to understand why our father hated George. My father and I didn't hate each other, which made George feel I was taking sides against him. This hurt him deeply. Our mother was a nothing—inadequate and just tried

141

to stay out of the way so as not to get caught in the crossfire between George and our father, who he called Arthur. I called him Dad.

"George was the most intelligent person I've ever known and nobody has been able to make me laugh the way he could when we were young. For a while, he liked to assemble model battleships and airplanes, but that led to his starting a brush-fire outside our house when he set fire to a couple of them and threw them out the window. I helped my father put the flames out, which hurt George terribly. When I got back to George's room a few hours later, he was sitting there in the dark on his bed, but he wasn't really there.

"Things got worse. He began to talk out loud to imaginary people. One day he did that in school—he shouldn't have been in school in the state he was in. The teacher got so frightened she took him to the school nurse who called for an ambulance that took him to the emergency room and they called our mother to tell her to meet him there. When I heard about it—kids were talking about it in the hallways—I ran out the front door of the school, and I remember the feeling I had as I stood there not knowing where he was. It felt like the end of the world. I ran home, which was a mile or so from the school, and no one was there. I called my father at work and he told me what happened, and said I should just stay at home until my mother got back from the hospital. They admitted him to a psychiatric ward. They wouldn't let me visit him.

"I went to George's room and cried and cried. I didn't get out of bed the whole time he was in the hospital. Everything looked pale gray. You'd think that with one child in a mental hospital and the other unable to get out of bed for a week or two, they'd take me to a psychiatrist, or maybe to our family doctor, but they didn't. They acted as if nothing unusual was happening. I've never felt as lonely as I did then. I went to school, read the books, passed the tests, but I didn't know who I was. I didn't know anything. I couldn't see colors. Everything looked like a black-and-white photo. I went to junior college and lived in a dive with some other students, but hardly said anything to anybody. I took some studio art classes, and began to draw again, which helped a lot. It was the fact that I could draw that got me into the university here.

"George was in and out of mental hospitals. He decided to join the Army. They were so desperate for bodies to send to Vietnam that they let him enlist. He didn't tell anybody he was doing this. He was nineteen, almost twenty. After two weeks in the Army, he decided he didn't like it, so he left, as if it were sleep-away camp. He was AWOL, and two MPs came to the house and arrested him for desertion. My parents did nothing, saying that the Army would get him a military lawyer who knew all about these things, and he'd straighten things out for George. I didn't believe it. I called law firms listed in the phone book, and they directed me to a group of anti-war lawyers who defended men pro bono who were trying to escape the draft or had deserted from the Army or got into some other kind of trouble. George was in a military prison in Elwin for a month while his anti-war defense attorney made the argument that the Army should never have allowed him to enlist in the first place given the number of times he'd been admitted to psychiatric hospitals. In order not to draw attention to the fact that they were so desperate to enlist men that they took any-one who could walk, the Army agreed to release George with a general discharge, not a dishonorable discharge.

"I'm going on and on. I'm thinking more about all of this than I have in a long time, and it's painful for me to remember these things. Are you sure you want to hear more?"

"Yes, I'm sure, go ahead."

"Dad died of a heart attack a few years after George's break-down, and my mother couldn't deal with anything having to do with George after that. For a year or so after his discharge from the Army, he lived at a custodial place that provided med-ications and not much else. I visited him there a few times, but he was so drugged up it was hard to feel there was a person there. When my mother said she couldn't afford to keep him in that facility any more, George was released. He stopped taking his medications and very soon broke down completely. He was hospitalized again. When I spoke to him by phone just before he was released, he said he just wanted to be left alone. When I asked him how he was going to do that, he surprised me by telling me he had a plan. It seemed completely unrealistic to me. He wanted to live in a VW van. The long and the short of it is that, for the past five or six years, he *has* lived in a van. My mother had enough money from my father's life insurance policy to cover the cost of the van and the way George has been living. He's spent the last few years driving all over the country, sleeping in the van, occasionally staying in 'economy motels' or B & Bs so he could take a shower. He uses public bathrooms in shopping centers and fast food restaurants or does it in the woods. I wire him money to the Western Union office he tells me to send it to. I've given him a stack of stamped addressed envelopes, and he just writes the name and location of the Western Union to send the money to, and maybe a few words more. He also calls me from pay phones late at night once in a while, just to hear my voice, or when he's feeling frightened or lonely or to ask me for help with a practical problem he's having.

"I don't know if you could tell, but he's still a remarkably sensitive guy. He can tell how I'm feeling, and asks me what's the matter when he hears something's not right with me by my tone of voice. And he can tell when something is right with me. Once he heard in my voice that I was feeling better than he'd heard me feeling in a very long time. That was right after I met you. I couldn't lie to him because he'd know if I was lying, and he'd get very upset and might act crazy and get himself hospitalized again, or worse, so I told him a little about you, and I reassured him that he wouldn't lose me because I had a girlfriend, that everything would be the same between us.

"Lately, he's heard in my voice that something's upsetting me. You may not believe this, but I firmly believe it: he came to the house to size you up, to see if you were a danger to me— maybe kill me—and he'd try to protect me if he thought you were dangerous. From what you've told me about the time you spent with him, he trusts you. I know that that isn't entirely reassuring because you're asking yourself, 'What if he changes his mind about me?'"

They sat in silence for a while before Madeline said, "Robert, you're a juggler with too many balls in the air: George, Charlie, Otto, Joe, the boss, your artwork, the anti-war movement, James-who-shot-himself-in-the-head—who may not have ever really existed but is a presence, a suicide threat, nonetheless— oh, and there's me. I'm just one more ball to juggle, aren't I?"

Robert was at a loss for words.

"No, you're not," he said. "How can I get that across to you? I love you. I've been wanting to tell you that, but have been afraid you'd feel I was making claims on you I had no right to make. But I want to say it before the worst happens."

"I feel sorry for George and sorry for you, but I don't want him as a fixture in my life—a deranged man who has nothing to do but frighten me and threaten you with suicide."

"I don't want you to feel sorry for me or see me as pathetic. Who wants a pathetic guy who works at a gas station? I feel pathetic sometimes, but most of the time I don't. I bring a lot of baggage with me that I felt I had to keep secret from you. And now that you know about all of it, it sounds like you're preparing yourself, and me, for the end of us."

The couch was in almost complete darkness now that the remnants of dusk coming through the windows had died away. Madeline was not untouched by Robert's telling her he loved her—the first man, other than her father, to tell her that. But she mistrusted Robert. He'd lied to her—as she did to him, she had to admit. "I don't know what to say. I understand how important you and George are to one another, but I'm not sure

145

there's any room for me or anyone else in that world the two of you live in. And even if there were room for me, I'm not sure I'd want to live in it."

"I'm so sorry about what George put you through today. It was cowardly of me not to protect you from him by telling you about him and the possibility that he might show up the way he did. He's never attacked anyone. You must have been able to feel that when you were with him."

"After his Big Bad Wolf entry, I felt pretty sure he wasn't going to physically assault me, but he did emotionally assault me. I'm not a doctor in an insane asylum who gets paid for doing that."

"But can't you be compassionate?"

"I don't know that I can."

TWENTY

George was childlike in the simplicity and ineptitude of his methods of stalking Madeline, to the point where it would have been endearing had it been a game played by a ten-year-old with his mother. He hid behind cars in a supermarket parking lot as Madeline put groceries into the trunk of her car, and he sat on the steps of the library most of an afternoon waiting for her to push the glass door with her shoulder as she emerged carrying her books and manila folders. Though Robert assured Madeline that George was harmless, they both knew it was possible, maybe probable, that George would become violent if he thought that she was a danger to Robert. Madeline told Robert that she felt the sting of George's eyes on her every minute of the day and night.

One evening, Madeline was fuming as she waited for Robert to return to the house after he closed the gas station for the night. Before he had time to take off his jacket, she said sternly, "There's something I have to talk to you about, *now*." He followed her into the kitchen where they took seats on opposite sides of the table.

"A student in my section of Western Civ came up to me today just as the class was gathering and whispered in my ear quietly, so no one else could hear, 'Do you know there's a homeless man standing in the hallway outside this room?'

"I felt humiliated. A homeless man! I felt like the stench of his body was all over me. I went out into the hallway and said to George, 'Please leave the building and leave me alone. I promise you I'll call the police and have you arrested if you don't leave this second. Am I getting through to you?' He looked so frightened and confused, I doubt he understood a word I said. I told him and I'm telling you, I will not tolerate being stalked. Get him the fuck off of me and away from my classes. Am I being clear enough to you?

"Get him out of my life—now!" she continued, screaming in his face. "I can feel his presence every second. He might as well be at the window looking in at me. It's driving me crazy! Do you have any idea what it feels like to be stalked by an insane, filthy man who could kill you if he gets it in his head to do it?"

"Madeline, I'm sorry that he's …"

"I don't care if you're sorry. Your being sorry is of no use to me. I have worked very hard to achieve the standing I have in the English Department and I will not have that undermined by your brother. Put a stop to it now. Go out into the woods, pick him up by the scruff of his neck, and tell him to leave me alone." Madeline put her face in her hands and wept while shaking her head.

Robert leaned forward to comfort her, but she took one of her hands from her face and motioned him away. Flushed with anger, she looked across the table at him and said through her teeth, "You may find that working at a gas station—probably a money-laundering operation—and living in a house behind it suits you, but it doesn't suit me. I've worked hard for years to escape the cesspool my parents inhabited, and I've come a long way. I will not sit by and watch myself dragged down into a pit by you and your brother. When I see my classes being invaded by this insane, wretched man, it feels to me like you're standing there next to him. If you can't control him and rid my life of him, it's the end of our relationship. I will not tolerate it.

148

I have never given you an ultimatum like this, so please believe I mean it."

As these words were coming from her mouth, Madeline felt a chill of fear running down her spine, for Robert had been the steady force that kept her sane and relatively calm. He had been the foundation on which she'd built all that she was telling him she would not part with.

As she looked at him across the table, she felt that she had been wrong to remain silent about the fact that Robert had been working at the gas station for a long time—he was always vague about the number of years he'd been working there—and that he had created a little world for himself there, a world that asked almost nothing of him, while she was pursuing an academic career.

Madeline said in a composed tone, "I have to be honest with you. When you and I were at the reception at the home of the chairman of the English Department—what was that, a month or two ago?—I was afraid someone might ask you what kind of work you do, and that you would say, 'I work at a gas station.' I know I'm a snob for feeling this way, but I don't want to spend my life with a gas station attendant. It sounds harsh, but that's the way I feel. Your brother's 'visit' has brought all of this to a head for me. I don't think you know the depth of shame I felt when that student told me there was a homeless man standing outside my classroom. I know your brother is a tortured soul whose insanity is a life sentence handed him when he was just an innocent boy. But you've taken it upon yourself to be your brother's keeper, and now it's your responsibility to deal with that fact."

Robert looked over at her, locking his eyes on hers, and said, "I know my brother is insane, and I will do what needs to be done to get him out of our lives. But you must be aware that that's not what bothers me most about what you've just said. Does my art really count for nothing to you? Do you see me as

149

a man who has delusions of grandeur? A poseur? Is that what you think? Is it?"

Each of Robert's words landed a blow. Madeline had never once, either at the reception or now in this "conversation," thought of Robert as an artist. She genuinely liked some of his artwork and admired his devotion to art, she said to herself, but he was right in saying that she didn't take his art seriously, that she didn't take him seriously as an artist. She thought this might be because he was so isolated as an artist, cut off from more experienced painters and sculptors who might critique his artwork, help him to grow as an artist. But the fact was she thought of him as a gas station attendant. Why had it not occurred to her at the reception and now at the "house behind the gas station"—as both she and Robert referred to this place—that if someone at the reception had asked him about himself, he might have responded with dignity, "I have a day job at a service station, but what I'm actually doing with my life is trying to develop as an artist"? She had somehow pushed out of mind the fact that every evening—sometimes deep into the night—and half of each day of every weekend, he was immersed in art. She'd treated his artwork as a hobby, something that held no value for her or the people in the world in which she lived. The fact that he had no stature in the art world—no gallery representing him, no academic position—made him, in her mind, a nobody. She felt deeply ashamed of her coldness, her pretentiousness.

She said, "I know that words spoken cannot be unsaid, but I'm very sorry I demeaned you. I was doing what I hate most in myself—I was being cruel, a mindless snob. I know this will sound empty, but I greatly respect you as an artist. I've never put this to myself in this way, but I have often felt it: I *study* literature; I don't create literature. I teach English; I'm not a novelist or a poet. You're an artist, you create art, you do art, and you do it well, and you're learning all the time how to be an artist, while I'm only learning how to teach other people's art.

It was a horrible, horrible thing to say, and I apologize to you. I know that that doesn't undo what I did."

Robert wept as he listened to Madeline. She reached across the table holding her hand out to his, but he didn't put his hand on hers.

"What you just said is the nightmare I live with all the time," Robert said. "It would be obvious to anyone who knew about us that you deserve better than me, and I feel certain that you will have better than me. I don't know what you're doing with someone like me. And the last straw, and I didn't anticipate this, is my schizophrenic brother who is unwashed and foul-smelling, lives in his van, and is utterly lost in this world. I've been afraid that if you ever knew about him, much less saw him, you'd want to get as far from me as you could. And that's what's happened. I don't want to lose you, but in a way it would be a relief if you left now because I think it's inevitable. I don't want to spend my life with George—I want to spend it with you. But I don't want to waste your time, have you spend your twenties with a man you couldn't possibly marry."

Madeline wished she could assure Robert that it was untrue that she found him unsuitable in the ways he described, but she couldn't.

Robert couldn't sleep that night. He hoped being by himself outside might help. He paced the length of the gas station. A soft breeze brushed his flushed face while words Madeline had spoken ran through his head. He felt as if Madeline's ordering him to get George out of their lives was like telling him to cut off his right arm—an unthinkable thing to ask of anyone. And at the same time, he felt as if George had stolen his right arm, and that he had to muster the courage to retrieve it from him, for he needed it, he had to get it back if he was to live an ordinary life. Talking to himself—at times silently, at times out loud—he spoke in fury to Madeline, to George, to himself; he couldn't stop.

151

He wrote a note to George—"Let's meet. When, where?"—and put it in the frozen orange juice can that he and George used as a method of communicating when George was nearby. George refused to use the phone during the rare times he visited Robert; who knew why?—probably not even George. Robert would leave the frozen juice can in the designated place next to the road just beyond the south edge of the gas station, and George would come by, usually in the early hours of the morning, read the note, and write his response on the other side of the piece of paper. This method of exchanging notes felt mad but practical to Robert.

He returned to the house and lay on the living room couch until 5:00. Robert then put on his shoes, grabbed a coat, and walked in his boxers to the place where he'd left the can. Relieved to see that the can had been moved a few feet from where he had left it, Robert picked it up and read George's response, penciled in child-like printing: *Food. Ten, am*" which was code for the diner at 10:00 a.m.

Just before 10:00, Robert arrived at the diner and waited for an hour and fifteen minutes—sitting in one of the booths, cracking his knuckles, looking out of the window at the parking lot, sipping lukewarm coffee. The waitresses sensed that he was upset as he waited. Audrey had offered him fresh coffee, which he declined. Now, at 11:15, he sank into a state of resignation to the fact that he had absolutely no power over George. He wished George had never been born.

Robert was so firmly in the grip of his thoughts that the sight of George forcing open the inner glass door to the diner came as a surprise. George looked even worse than he had when Robert last saw him; how many years ago was that?—he didn't even want to try to figure that out. George was a tall, full-grown man, not the vibrant teenage boy that Robert kept in his mind.

As George walked down the aisle between the counter seats and the booths, he placed his left hand on the edge of each bench, trying to maintain his balance. He was very thin, unshaven, his hair greasy, his clothes filthy, his pants baggy. Ordinarily, a homeless man would be escorted outside to the back of the diner where he would be given some discarded food and told not to come back, but the waitresses knew this man was Robert's brother and pretended not to notice him.

George gave Robert a warm but sad smile.

"Sorry I'm late."

"That's all right."

"Today?"

"Yeah," Robert said, not understanding George's question and refusing to try to understand.

"Bobby, do you think they'd give me just fries?"

"Yeah."

Robert gave George's order and his own to Audrey, who was now standing by their table. She was careful not to look directly at George.

When their food arrived, Robert watched as George covered his French fries with a thick layer of ketchup, and then pushed his fingers through the ketchup to take two or three fries at a time and stuffed them into his mouth, leaving a smear of ketchup between his upper lip and nose.

"She wanted to murder me," George said.

"Who wanted to murder you?"

"Don't play dumb. You know who."

"Madeline?"

"Yeah, I don't like the name. Stuck-up, don't you think?"

"Did she say she wanted to murder you?"

"She said it with her eyes."

Robert was tongue-tied.

"You want to murder me too, don't you Bobby?"

"No, I don't."

"Then why the angry note?"

"I wasn't angry, I just wanted to talk."

"I'm not stupid, Bobby."

"All right. Let's start again," Robert said.

"Impossible. But say whatever you have to say."

"All right. Why did you tell Madeline about James?"

"I don't know why. I just did. Why shouldn't I?"

"Because … I don't know. Because we're the only ones who knew him and care about what happened to him."

"Arthur killed him," George said.

"He killed himself."

"You're smarter than that. He shot himself, but Arthur had already killed him. We watched it happen. She watched."

"Who?"

"God damn it, Bobby. You know who I mean. Why are you playing dumb? I swear to God I'll never *just watch*, never."

"Watch what?"

"Jesus Christ! Who are you? You were a smart kid, Bobby, really smart. We made a promise to look after each other. You promised you'd never let anything happen to me like what happened to James, and I promised I'd never let anything happen to you. You remember."

"Sure, I remember …"

"But what?" George said, raising his voice, staring hard at Robert.

Robert sat there like a stutterer unable to get the words from his mouth.

"But what, Bobby!"

"Shushhh … You can't do that here."

"Don't shush me. Answer me! But what?"

"But I don't want you to come to the house again the way you did or follow Madeline around … or come to the place where I live without my permission."

"Finally! That's what you've been wanting to say the whole time—that's why you wanted to talk to me. What do you want from me?"

"I told you. I want you to give me your word that you won't come to the town or area where I'm living without telling me first and getting my permission, and in particular, never follow Madeline around ever again. I know you're trying to protect me, like we promised each other, but you've checked her out now. She's harmless." Robert hesitated before adding, "And this last thing: she's the first real girlfriend I've had, so you're going to have to let me take care of myself on this one … Do you understand?"

"I don't know, Bobby."

"Will you give me your word that you won't come to the house unless I'm there, and you won't …"

"I know, I know. How many times do you have to say it?"

"Will you give me your word on it?"

"My 'word'? I'll give you my word: fuck you. That's two words. You can keep the change." George's eyes were welling with tears.

"George, you and I are brothers. I'd never let anyone or anything come between us, I really wouldn't. You know me better than anyone and you know I couldn't do that to you."

Tears were now running down George's cheeks.

"I know. I didn't know, but I know now," George said.

After sitting there together quietly for a few minutes, George slowly took a few napkins from the napkin dispenser, dipped them in the glass of water in front of him, and slowly washed the ketchup off his fingers.

TWENTY-ONE

Very early, the windows still black, Robert heard loud clanking sounds coming from the kitchen. Turning to see if Madeline was in bed next to him, he was surprised to see just sheets and blanket where her body should be. He got out of bed and walked into the living room. He could see Madeline in a green T-shirt and gray sweatpants leaning over the kitchen sink scrubbing, her elbows in commotion, like turkey wings flapping.

"I've been up all night wanting to talk with you," she said, looking at Robert across the room, "but I couldn't get myself to wake you in the middle of the night, because there's nothing I hate more than looking desperate. So I've been pretending to be doing the dishes and knocking the pots and pans together in hopes of waking you up."

Robert smiled.

Madeline, a bit calmer, said, "Can we sit down so I can try to say what I have to say?"

"All right."

Once they were seated at the kitchen table, Madeline said, "It's taken a couple of days for me to feel the full impact of the horrible things I said to you. About feeling ashamed of you, not wanting to be seen with you, calling you a gas station attendant, and on top of that, leaving out the fact that you work very hard and very well as an artist, and you want very much to be recognized and valued as an artist by the art world, and by me.

"You know me. I have trouble apologizing for anything, even awful, damaging things I've said or done.

"Since we had that conversation—it wasn't a conversation, it was a bullying session—I haven't been able to sleep. I've been nauseated by what I did. Things have changed. I've changed. Being with you has changed me. Once, I wouldn't even have noticed I'd behaved the way I did with you. I could actually put it out of my mind as if it never happened. But now I can't forget in that way. I can't forget what I did to you; I don't want to forget it. It's a fact, it happened, and I have to, I want to, take responsibility for it. Since we talked, I've been frightened that you'll leave me and I don't want that, but I know it could happen. That you'll decide you don't want to be around someone like me."

Madeline paused, afraid she was using too many words. Robert was silent, his eyes fixed on the yellow vinyl tablecloth in front of him.

After a while, she continued, "I know that both of us are aware of something but have never talked about it. We both know that you've told me you love me, and I've never said that to you. It was out of cowardice that I've never told you I love you. I've been too afraid to expose myself to you. But I do love you, and I'm so sorry I hurt you the way I did."

Madeline paused and reached over to pat Robert's hand, which was lying flat on the table. He didn't pull his hand from hers. She straightened up and continued. "I accused you of betraying me by keeping George a secret from me. I believed it when I said it, which now seems absurd. I admire your devotion to George. I know that he was once a different person, and you loved him very much, and now that he's terribly ill, you still love him and care for him. How could I have begrudged you your choice to keep George out of our life as a couple? We've been kind to one another in not extracting anything from the other one, and allowing each other to keep secret what we will, until we want to say it. There are things I want to tell you that I've kept secret because I'm ashamed of them and have been afraid you'll see me as sick, insane. I want you to know what I've been keeping from you because you have to know it if you're going to really know who I am and what you've gotten yourself into. It is hard for me to say out loud …"

Robert lifted his head and said, "Madeline, this may not be the time to tell me what you've been afraid to say. It might feel like you're telling me because you want to try to make up for having said what you said. Maybe you should wait."

"No, I can't wait. I want to tell you now that being with you has changed me in a fundamental way, changed something that began happening to me when I was a young girl. I don't know precisely when it started happening because I thought that everyone was like this—but it got a lot worse when my parents were breaking up. What I'm trying to say is I have thoughts that don't feel like my own—thoughts that scold me, instruct me, denigrate me. You've seen me so confused I don't know who I am. The first thing I did when I met you was to ask you for directions to the blood bank. I was in some other reality. And then I walked out of the administration building because I didn't know what I was doing there. Since I moved in with you, I've only had those demeaning thoughts—those voices—once in a while. They've almost gone away because you calm me, make me feel loved and accepted as I am, which takes a lot of power away from the voices. You have no idea what a gift that is, and I've never thanked you for it because I couldn't tell you they've been there and how confused I get, how crazy I feel."

Madeline got up, walked around the table and pulled the side of Robert's head to her. She said, "I'm really sorry and I promise it won't happen again."

Robert stood, put his arms around Madeline, and said, "I forgive you."

"So we're good?"

"Yeah, we're good, we're very good."

TWENTY-TWO

Robert could remember every detail of the moment he heard that JFK had been shot and killed in Dallas on the 22nd of November 1963—the dim lighting in the school hallway in which he was standing between classes in the early afternoon, the face of the student who, with tears running down his face, told him what had happened, the ache of the wish that it wasn't true, and the profound sorrow of knowing it was true and there was no reversing it. Neither would he ever forget the moment on Monday, the 4th of May in 1970 when Charlie, not long after they'd had their lunch break, opened the door to the office, his face creased with sadness, said, "They've shot and killed four students … marching … Ohio, I think. It's on the radio … Well, I just wanted to tell you."

"They killed them, not just shot them?"

"Yeah."

"What a fucking thing, Charlie."

Robert left the office and rushed back to the house to watch the news on the TV he stored on the floor next to the couch. Before he could begin setting it up, he staggered to the bathroom, and vomited into the toilet. On leaving the bathroom after rinsing his mouth, he was shivering, the house felt unreal to him, as if he were entering someone else's home, a place filled with someone else's things.

Lifting the television and pressing it into his chest with his left arm, he used his forearm to swipe across the surface of the work table, sending drawings, brushes, glass jars flying all over the room. He lowered the bulky television onto the table and plugged it into the extension cord at his feet. Robert stood over the machine, impatiently repositioning the rabbit ear antenna, trying to clear the flickering black-and-white snow in which he could discern faintly human shapes. It took a few minutes to get the rabbit ears into the right position to pick up the weak signal.

When, finally, the television was able to pick up images and sounds, Robert was confronted by more than he could have imagined. The television cameras were panning over a large open, flat area where he could make out small human figures. The camera, or maybe it was another camera, then focused, in sequence, on one dead body after the other, each surrounded by four or five students, one of whom, a girl in shock, was screaming for help, or screaming in agony, though no sound was being transmitted. The television reporter was silent for a minute or more as the camera moved from one body to the next.

Robert watched the tape of the events leading to the killings: A group of several hundred students were filmed chanting, "Strike, strike, strike," as sixty or seventy soldiers carrying bayonet rifles ran to take positions on three sides of the group. A soldier through a bullhorn ordered the protestors to disperse. Robert could hear the pop of tear gas canisters fired into the group of protestors. Some of the students picked up the canisters and threw them back at the Ohio National Guardsmen. Seemingly for no reason at all, a few rifle shots could be heard, and a second or two later, volleys of rifle shots that seemed to go on forever were fired at the protestors. The camera jumped from one part of the scene to another as the wounded and dead protestors lay sprawled on the ground, while other protestors fled in the direction of the adjoining sports field. A renewed volley of shots was fired at the fleeing students. Still other protestors, despite the continued rifle fire, stayed on the university's Commons area to tend to the wounded and dead.

Robert kept watching these same scenes and listening to the drone of the voice of the reporter. Intermittently, bits of new information were announced. In addition to the four students who were killed, nine others had been seriously wounded and had been taken to a nearby hospital. Two of the four students killed were not protestors, but were merely walking between classes. Students interviewed said that this was a relatively peaceful demonstration compared with the one earlier in the week, at the end of which the protestors had burnt to the ground the ROTC building.

The anchor solemnly, disapprovingly, read from an anti-war speech Jerry Rubin, a national leader of the anti-war movement, had given at Kent State six weeks earlier: "The first part of the program is to kill your parents. They are the first oppressors."

Robert walked stiffly to the kitchen to get a glass of water. As he stood by the sink, his body felt numb, his lips bloated, his hand on the water glass felt gloved. A line had been crossed. He returned to his chair at the work table and turned off the sound, but not the images on the screen.

As Robert continued to watch the clips of the protestors being shot, he felt clearly now, for the first time, the full ferocity of shame he had managed to keep at bay all these years. He felt his face flush as he thought about the way he had disgraced himself by passively allowing himself to be sent into exile. He had created and maintained for years a position for himself—in quite a literal way—at the side of a steep hill, atop of which stood the university. He'd neutered himself, made himself harmless.

Robert was so completely in the grip of these feelings that he didn't hear Madeline come in the front door. He startled when he felt a soft, cold hand on his neck. She seemed part of a world he recalled but no longer occupied.

163

"I heard about Kent State. I ..."

"Sit down with me, would you, in the kitchen," Robert said. He walked across the room and Madeline followed.

"Madeline, this isn't just a horrible news event for me. It carries with it something deeply personal for me. I'm not sure what to do. I've been sitting here having grandiose thoughts about going up there to the campus and assuming the role I held years ago, as a young student, leading a demonstration or a sit-in or something. But the reality is that time has passed up there without me.

"I've had some ridiculous thoughts. I've imagined bringing the television up there and setting it up on the Quad where the activists used to gather and we'd exchange ideas, make plans, dream things up. I thought about bringing long, industrial-strength extension cords and hooking up the TV to electricity through a dorm room window. Don't laugh, the idea actually occurred to me. I want to go, I have to go, to the campus and take part in whatever response there is to what happened today, but I don't want to make a fool of myself. In particular, I don't want to presume to hold a place, to play a role I've long since given up."

Madeline, sensing that Robert was getting stuck in his own thoughts, said, "It's not as if you have any choice about this."

It felt strange to Robert to be driving up the hill for a purpose other than picking up or dropping off Madeline. He had no standing at the university. He had no right to be there, no right to park his car in the south parking lot.

On walking up the slight rise of the path that had blocked his view of the Quad, Robert found a group of about fifty students and a few older people who may have been professors or administrators. He felt awkward as he stood on the grass outside the five curved stone benches that were placed around a war memorial—a circular bronze piece, three or four feet in diameter, on which were engraved the names of alumni killed in the Second World War. The Latin words *HINC ILLAE LACRIMAE* were printed above the names along the curve of the upper rim: "Hence these tears."

Not knowing what to do, Robert walked around the campus. He passed students listening to transistor radios in groups, others walking alone seemingly aimlessly holding radios to their ear, still others seated on the ground, their backs against one of the dark red brick buildings surrounding the Quad. The sky was the same bleak gray as the sky at Kent State he'd seen on TV. What was striking was that virtually no one was speaking; neither were they in physical contact with one another—no one had their arms draped on another's shoulders, there were no handshakes, no pats on the back. Many had tears running down their cheeks; many had lost, blank expressions on their faces.

Robert felt like a ghost returning to a place where he had once belonged, but from which he was banned and then banned himself. Having made his way, seemingly invisible, around parts of the sprawling campus, he returned to the war memorial at the center of the Quad, the place where he felt least out of place. Robert could feel someone on the other side of the war memorial staring at him. When he lifted his gaze to see who it was, he saw a young man wearing wire-rimmed glasses. This student, who looked no more than nineteen, walked around the memorial and approached Robert, put out his hand, and said, "You're Robert Renfro, aren't you?"

Robert, taken by surprise, shook his hand and said, "I am. I'm sorry to be rude. Have we met?"

"Yes, I was a freshman the last year you were here. I'm a grad student now."

"What's your name?"

"Brian Kaufman."

Robert looked hard at him.

"I was a freshman the year you were expelled and they shut down SDS. I took a few years off at the end of that year.

165

When I got back, the place had turned into a world separate from everything outside. There have been sporadic efforts to get an anti-war movement going, but they've failed before they got started. There's a small group of students who might be interested in doing something now. We need someone to help us if anything's going to happen now."

"I think you have an inflated view of me," Robert said.

"I'm sorry to put you on the spot this way, but I don't know what else to do."

Robert was silent.

"Would you be willing to meet with a few of us?"

"When?"

"In a couple of hours. Let's say six … in front of Archer Hall?"

Finding himself alone again at the war memorial at the center of the Quad, he watched the students milling around. They looked different. Styles had changed from when he was a student. The girls' hair was longer now—shoulder-length or all the way down their back. A lot of them wore ankle-length dresses with a jacket or sweater. Frayed jeans and T-shirts with swirling purplish colors seemed to be in fashion. The conversation he'd had with Brian left him uneasy. It wasn't a conversation really. Leading a group was something he'd once done, but he felt old for it now. He didn't belong here now.

As the students arrived at Archer Hall, Brian made the introductions. About fifteen showed up. They all looked very young, maybe eighteen or nineteen. The air had become cold all of a sudden. Brian led the group to a seminar room with enough chairs for everyone, but not so large as to dwarf the group.

Robert took a seat on one side of the long wooden table in the center of the room. Brian stood at the front of the room, and motioned with his hand to Robert that he should begin the meeting. Robert was surprised by the rapidity with which he was being cast as leader of this group. Not knowing what else to do, he stood and said, "I'm Robert Renfro, a newcomer … or more accurately, a latecomer to this group. I'm here to help with whatever you have in mind to do."

Brian would have nothing of it. "Let's not get caught up in deferring to one another. What we need to do now is plan a response to what happened at Kent State. Robert, tell us what we have to do to make some sort of protest happen."

It was hard for Robert to read the faces of the students gathered around the table. Some of them seemed to want to get down to work; others looked as if they'd found themselves in the wrong classroom and planned to leave as soon as the moment presented itself.

"All right, I'll do that," Robert said, "but you all have to understand that there's a hell of a lot to do if there's going to be an organized demonstration four days from now. If I find I'm working on my own, I'm out of here."

During the four hours that followed, a group of a dozen or so planned a march that would gather in the town square and march up the hill to the campus and then down to the Quad, a distance of about a quarter mile. Subgroups of three or four were each delegated responsibility for different aspects of what needed to be done. When the meeting broke up, Robert drove back to the house and left a note for George in the orange juice can: *I'm safe. march on Friday evening. no soldiers.*

Robert, before returning to the campus, made himself a peanut butter sandwich, which he ate with a bottle of beer, after which he leaned back in his chair and let out a long, satisfying belch that felt like it came from the center of him—a tribute of sorts to the big brother he once had.

Robert spent the nights of that week in one of the vacant dormitory rooms, but hardly slept. Sleeping in one of the same dormitories where he'd lived when he was a student brought back memories that deeply pained him. Like a closed loop of feeling repeating itself in his mind, he relived the shame of being duped by the Weather Underground and by his own vanity, his so quickly crumbling under pressure from the dean, and his silently crawling into a hole at the side of the road leading up to the campus.

TWENTY-THREE

The days that followed were exhausting. The students working on the preparations for the march at first seemed dazed by the prospect of dealing with the real world—getting permits from the university and from the town police, arranging for sound and lighting equipment and for the construction of a wooden platform in the Quad, seeing to it that the event was covered by the local newspaper, printing flyers and distributing them, and on and on. Robert lost track of time as he worked, lost track of George and Madeline, lost track of when he last had a meal.

The day of the march, Robert made his way to the town square around 5:00, a half hour before the march was to begin. The sky was a deep blue, the air unusually warm for early May. As he walked down the soft slope of the road from the campus to the square, he could see hundreds of people of all ages gathering.

He recognized many of the people as he meandered around the square, mostly professors he'd had who were standing there with their families. It seemed to him that he could see them, but they could not see him.

It was now 5:30. The crowd that had gathered, perhaps four or five hundred in all, overflowed the square. Robert and the group that had helped put together this event began the march up the hill to the north entrance of the university. Dusk was beginning to settle in.

The marchers were quiet as they walked. It took about twenty minutes for the group to climb to a position from which Robert could see the bright lights from the Quad, a hundred yards ahead. It appeared to be half full already, and clearly would be overfilled by those marching behind him. A group of fifteen or twenty men yelling obscenities at the approaching marchers were being pushed to the side by the police and campus security.

A platform of three levels of wooden planks held together with metal scaffolding stood at the north edge of the Quad, about twenty-five yards from the war memorial that stood at its center. Campus security helped make space for those arriving from the town square. Robert had struggled with what he was going to say when the whole group assembled in the Quad, never feeling he'd gotten it right.

Standing on the middle tier of the platform in back of a metal stand on which the microphone was held, he began. "I'm overwhelmed by the number of people assembled here. I spent many hours preparing my opening remarks for this gathering. I will not be using much of what I wrote because I've learned so much from all of you, young and old, as you've gathered here this evening. I've learned from the solemnity, the formality, the gravity with which you've conducted yourselves. There isn't a poster to be seen or an anti-war chant to be heard. You've taught me that we're not here to protest the burning alive of men, women, and children with napalm in Vietnam, the genocide being conducted in our name, the mass graves we see on the evening news every night. There will be other nights to raise our voices to protest those atrocities.

"Tonight we have gathered because we cannot bear being alone with the grief we're feeling in response to the events at Kent State four days ago. Our gathering is a memorial for the four people senselessly shot to death at Kent State: Allison

170

Krause, nineteen years old; Jeffrey Miller, twenty years old; Sandra Scheuer, twenty years old; and William Schroeder, nineteen years old. We've seen film clips that record the horror of it—an unthinkable blotting out of life.

"Each of the four who were killed has a family that is suffering the worst that life has to dish out, the death of a child—a depth of pain that is impossible for me to imagine.

"And nine other protestors were shot, not fatally, though one suffered a severed spinal cord. These young people who were not fatally shot are not 'all right,' as the newscasters insist they are. The wounded students are *not okay*. How can they ever again be *okay* after having heard the sound of volleys of rifle fire of sixty soldiers aiming their bayonet rifles at them, having felt the physical and emotional pain of a bullet entering their bodies, having felt the terror of dying of that wound, of having peered through clouds of tear gas at someone dead on the ground not far away, knowing there was nothing to protect them from being shot a second or a third time by the next rounds of bullets. How could they live through what they've experienced and be *okay*?

"And there are the other protestors at Kent State who were neither killed nor wounded. They will never be free of the memory of fleeing as the rifle fire continued to kill, as they watched the bodies of thirteen students fall to the ground either dead or wounded. That terror will never leave them. They're called the lucky ones, but there's nothing at all lucky about what they've been through. They're *not okay*.

"And none of us here is okay after having witnessed the events at Kent State. What has happened has changed us. We will never be the same, nor do we want to be the same as we were before. It is our responsibility *not* to be the same, *not* to be okay after having witnessed the events that occurred at Kent State earlier this week. And it is our responsibility to do something with our feeling of not being okay with those events."

171

Robert paused, not knowing how long he'd been speaking, but feeling he'd said everything he'd wanted to say. His gaze had been wandering around the crowd in front of him, not stopping to focus on anyone or anything. But he was listening to himself and, surprisingly, he felt that what he was saying was right for the occasion and right for him.

"Now let's have a minute's silence, which is more or less the length of time the rifle shots tore through the air at Kent State four days ago, a minute that must have felt interminable to those under fire."

Others spoke and sang from the platform. By 7:30 the crowd had dwindled to about half its original size. Families with young children had gone home some time ago. Robert could hear the voices of older children unable to stand still any longer, perhaps upset by seeing their parents cry.

Robert thanked everyone for taking part in the peaceful memorial event. A few men intent on undermining the calm of the gathering began belligerently bumping their shoulders hard against those exiting the Quad. A woman screamed, "Stop it!" Robert reached for the microphone, but in his haste knocked it over. When it hit the plank floor of the platform, the microphone let out a deep-throated boom and a screech.

There followed, only ten or fifteen seconds later, the sound of a blast that shook the windows of the buildings surrounding the Quad as the sound waves ricocheted from one building to another. Then a second explosion, and a third. The crowd stood frozen in shock, and then panic began to take hold.

Robert spoke calmly into the microphone. "What we're hearing is nothing more than fireworks. There are no soldiers shooting at us. We will only do violence to ourselves if we try to push our way out." Robert stayed at the microphone, speaking in a composed tone of voice until the last of those assembled had exited the Quad. This was not the ending that Robert had imagined.

As he stood there in the Quad, which was now empty of all but a dozen or so people, Robert felt certain it was George who had thrown the cherry bombs, as he had done so many times during their childhood. The sound of the blast was as familiar to him as George's voice.

TWENTY-FOUR

In semi-darkness, four men in their late thirties or early forties were now disassembling the wood planks and scaffolding while Robert and three other men were disconnecting the lighting and sound equipment. They moved slowly, like members of a symphony orchestra disassembling their instruments and carefully placing them in felt-lined cases after a performance. The men spoke quietly to one another. Then the squeal of tires on a car braking, followed by a dull thud and the sound of shattering glass, cut through the dark night air.

Robert lowered to the ground the amplifier he was carrying and ran the hundred yards or so toward the south entrance where the sound seemed to be coming from. He was stopped there by three campus security guards who were polite but firm in telling him that no one was allowed down the road.

The moon was three-quarters full, casting an eerie blue-white light that lit the south parking lot and surrounding buildings. A group of twenty or so students stood behind the row of red pylons that the campus security guards had set up. The sound of the static of police radios reminded Robert of static he'd heard the nights the police came to the house to take George to the emergency room when he was being tortured by the people who lived inside his head.

175

Robert retreated into the campus and made his way to the start of the trail along the top of the ridge that led to the gas station. By moonlight, he picked his way through the brush and low branches toward the site of the crash. After about ten minutes, he arrived at a point from which he could see a stretch of road brightly lit by the headlights of cars and trucks and by lights on metal stands. A man lay on a gurney positioned at the rear doors of an ambulance. A car must have driven off the side of the road into the ravine. Kneeling on the damp ground, feeling like a voyeur, Robert watched.

He felt certain it was George who lit the fireworks in a deluded effort to protect his kid brother. Or was it out of anger? Was it possible, he wondered, that George had done something to cause the car to veer off the road? Could he have stood in the road with the intention of causing the car to veer to the left into the gulley? Or, even more perverse, could he have poured gasoline or something else on the road, causing the car to skid and crash?

Robert now felt an urgent need to return to the house and somehow reach George. Hurrying along the trail toward the house, Robert pushed aside the branches of trees and bushes, some of which snapped back lashing his face. Before entering the house, he wrote a note that he put in the orange juice can: *must meet. where. when?*

After turning on the lights, he sat down on a kitchen chair to catch his breath and gather himself. He felt swallowed up by the terror that George had actually caused the death of someone, or perhaps several people, in that car.

George, he thought, was probably hiding in his van somewhere. He could be sent to prison, or more likely, to a facility for the criminally insane.

Robert remained seated at the kitchen table—the rest of the house illuminated only by the kitchen light. It was after midnight when he looked up at the clock over the sink. Too late to call Madeline, who'd been sleeping at a friend's apartment this week. There was nothing for him to do but wait—wait for George to respond to the note; wait for the morning newspaper to report the crash and the number injured or dead; wait for the police to knock on the door of his house to question him about what he knew about the explosions; wait for them to ask him about George; wait for the FBI to question him about the money-laundering operation at the gas station.

Robert found himself standing next to his work table, feeling no desire to sit or lie down because there was no place in the house—or in the world, for that matter—that he felt was his home. This house behind the gas station felt like a place where he had wasted his life, a place where he never wanted to spend another night. He remained standing in the midst of what felt like suffocating clutter.

Not knowing what else to do, Robert went to check the can once again. This time he found a note saying *Regular 7 am*. After writing *OK* after George's words, he pushed the paper deep into the can, feeling fed up with this game.

The cool, damp air stroked Robert's face as he stood by the side of the road breathing in the scent of the evergreens. His eyes stung and leaked tears. He walked to the office side of the gas station, where the light fixture in its metal cage cast its cold light.

Robert went to bed and tried to sleep, but after an hour, he decided to go outside again, where he stared up at the clear night sky filled with stars, letting his thoughts go where they would.

The familiar rusted green Rambler drove by, grumbling in first gear, as Randy Lungren flung from his open window a folded newspaper that skittered over the pavement for a yard or two before coming to rest some twenty-five feet in front of Robert. He picked it up and walked back to the area illuminated by the metal-caged light. His body was so tense, and his hands so cold and stiff, that he had difficulty unfolding the paper. There was a short column on the lower right of the front page of *The Valley Standard* under the headline, "Deadly Crash After University March."

(May 9, Reynolds, NY) A car careened off the side of Beckford Road in Reynolds at about 9:45 Friday night after an anti-war march at the university. The male driver was pronounced dead on arrival at Chautauqua County Hospital. The other three passengers were admitted to the hospital, their condition stable according to the hospital spokesman. Police are not releasing the names of the driver and passengers before next of kin are notified. The peaceful demonstration protesting the killing of four students by the Ohio National Guard drew between 800 and 1,000 people, according to police reports.

The sound of three loud explosions from the perimeter of the campus Quad led to the rapid dispersal of the demonstrators. Reynolds Police Chief, Aubrey Lent, said it is too early to determine the source of the three explosions or any connection between them and the car crash.

Robert read the brief article again and again, trying to wring from the words more than was there. For brief periods, Robert could believe that he was not responsible for the death of a man: all he did was lead a nonviolent march. But the calm that clung to that thought devolved into despair as Robert acknowledged to himself that he had not simply led a peaceful march; he had led the march knowing that his insane brother would conduct himself as his self-appointed guardian. He'd yearned so deeply for a new ending of a phase of his life that he'd minimized the threat that George posed.

As Robert stood with his back against the office door, he heard George's van come to a stop and park just down the hill from the gas station. He heard tentative footsteps approaching the usual place where the can was "hidden." Robert, speaking as softly and gently as he could, said, "George, I'm here. I'm not angry. Please let me get my car keys and follow you to a place where we can talk."

"Okay," George whispered.

Robert hurried back to the house for his keys, fearing that George would be gone by the time he got back. They drove— Robert in his car, close behind George's van—for about a half hour while George looked for a secure place where they could park. It was about 5:30 in the morning and the sky was brightening.

Finally, George pulled into the parking lot behind the county incinerator and parked his van in a corner out of sight from the street. Robert parked next to the van. About a minute later, George appeared in Robert's rear view mirror, looking more deranged and confused than the last time they'd met at the diner.

Robert slowly emerged from his car, and in a calm voice said, "George, it's all right. Please believe me, I'm not angry at you."

"Okay," George said in a tone of voice like that of a child waiting to be scolded.

"Where would you like to talk?"

"Right here." The parking lot stank of rotting garbage.

They were facing one another, Robert staring hard at George, while George stared through Robert's face, as if looking at something behind him.

"They're flying at me, Bobby."

"What's flying at you?"

"I don't know, they just are."

"Could we talk about the march?"

"I'd rather not."

"Could we anyway?"

"Yeah, I guess. They killed people at Kent State, didn't they?"

"There were police tonight, not National Guard troops like there were at Kent State." Robert felt he was in a place with George where logic didn't apply, where talking didn't help, where the problems facing them in the real world couldn't even be conceived of, much less discussed. Nothing could come of this, nothing was going to change, and Robert didn't think he could bear it any longer.

"They're all the same," George said, "don't you know that? They use different names—National Guard, ROTC, FBI, Police—but they're all the same. I was in the Army. I know about these things. You don't, you were never in the Army."

"George, slow down and just tell me what happened last night."

"It wasn't just last night."

"Let's stick to last night," Robert said, trying not to lose patience. "When all the people were in the Quad, what were you doing?"

"Watching."

"From where?"

"At the edge. Between the buildings."

"Did you light off cherry bombs? I know that sound from when we were kids, and I know they sell them around here."

"Only after the screaming and after the bomb went off."

"No bomb went off. There was a loud noise when I knocked over the microphone stand and the mike hit the platform floor. It's true that a woman screamed, but …"

"A bomb went off. It wasn't a microphone."

"So what did you do after the bomb went off?"

"There was a woman screaming like when JFK and Bobby Kennedy and Martin Luther King were shot."

"And then what did you do?"

"I don't know. I lit off the cherry bombs—not to hurt anyone. You know I would never do that. I just wanted to get their attention away from you so you could get away."

Robert stood there looking at George, not knowing what to say. George didn't know what had really happened. His mind was a collection of fragments of stories, swirling clouds of ideas, all of which were equally real, equally compelling.

After some time, Robert said, "George, please try to concentrate on what I'm going to say. I'll repeat it if you don't understand and I'll write it down in case you forget. Are you with me?"

"Yeah, but don't say something bad."

"No, it's not bad. First, I want you to always know that I will never cut you out of my life and leave you on your own. That's the most important thing. I'll never do that. I can't say that enough times. Got it?"

"Yeah, that's good."

"The other thing is that you have to let me have a life of my own. And I can't say that enough times either. Do you get that, really get it, not just say it and not mean it?"

"I didn't mean to scare her."

"George, forget about what happened with Madeline. It doesn't matter. What I want you to understand is that I don't want you living where I'm living."

"Never see me again?"

"No, I'm just asking you to tell me when you want to visit, and we'll have a visit. I want that."

"I do, too."

"And I want you to talk only to me when you visit. That's the harder part. Can you promise me you'll only talk with me when you visit?"

"Yeah, I can."

"That will be harder than you think because you think you have to protect me."

George didn't reply.

"George, that's the hard part, but you have to promise me you'll only talk to me and not try to protect me. Can you promise me that?" As Robert heard himself pleading with George, he realized George was incapable of keeping such a promise because reality was changeable for him, and in each new reality, old promises didn't apply. Everything was different.

"I promise. I can do that. I'm sorry. Sorry for everything."

Robert had decided not to talk to George about his fear that the police might want to talk to him about the explosions and the car crash. Nothing good could come of that. George would panic. Instead, he said to George, "I'm going back to my house and you'll be on your way to wherever you want to go. Okay?"

"Okay."

TWENTY-FIVE

Robert, on returning to the house after talking with George, knew he wouldn't be able to sleep, though he'd hardly slept the last four days—he didn't want to sleep. Somehow the hours of the day passed. Deep into the evening, he went to bed and fell asleep. On waking, he saw that the windows were brightly lit. He looked out the kitchen window and saw the back of the gas station. He looked at his watch and checked it against the clock in the kitchen; it was noon … on Sunday, though it didn't feel like Sunday.

Robert dressed and walked out to the area near the gas pump where he saw the fat Sunday newspaper, bloated with advertisements. He left it there and started walking up the road in the direction of the campus. He stood amidst the debris left behind by the police, the firemen, and the ambulance drivers: the burnt-out road flares, shards of mirror flickering in the dim sunlight, shattered pieces of red and orange plastic, a twisted fender, deep wheel ruts in the dirt, slabs of pavement hanging precariously over the ravine, torn pieces of pale blue medical paper and cellophane. He continued up the road.

As he walked, one of the dreams he had the previous night came to him—not as a memory, but as something real and immediate, as if it were happening now. The FBI, during their investigation of the crash, had happened upon the money-laundering operation at the gas station. Robert was being framed as the ringleader. The boss had disappeared. Then it was all over. The gas station and the house behind it were seized and everything was shut down. The mechanics were gone. Nothing remained. But what was most surprising of all was the fact that the dream ended—or maybe it was only now as he remembered the dream—the dream ended not with feelings of fear and dread about what was going to happen to him, or with sadness about all he'd lost—his job, his friends, his house, his studio. The dream ended with a vast feeling of relief. More than relief, he was thrilled by the freedom he felt.

When he reached the campus, Robert realized that it no longer felt like a place that was of any interest to him, so he turned and walked back down the road, passing a clearing where he could see bits of the path at the edge of the marshland where he and Madeline had had their first kiss.

As he opened the front door to the house, Madeline walked quickly from the kitchen and put her arms around him. "I've missed you. It's felt like a year, not a few days." She'd been staying with a friend in an off-campus apartment since Monday because she didn't like being in their house by herself at night.

"Madeline, so much has happened."

They sat down on the couch, Robert put his arm around her waist, and she laid her head on his shoulder.

"I don't know where to start. Were you still there when the three cherry bombs exploded?"

"No, I'd left by that time, but I heard people talk about the explosions. And it was on the local TV news."

"Well, as the demonstration was winding down, some goons began to give shoulder blows to people around them. A woman who was shoved screamed, 'Stop it,' and when I reached for the mike in its stand to try to calm things, the whole mike and stand fell over and made a loud booming and shrieking sound. You know what mikes sound like when they're dropped. Right after that came the explosions. You could feel the sound waves hit you as they bounced off the buildings around the Quad.

"George says he was trying to protect me by exploding the cherry bombs, but I don't think even he really knows why he did it. I knew immediately that it was George who'd done it, and I hated him for it. He was wrecking something that was important to me.

"I was up all night waiting for the paper to be delivered to find out if anyone had been killed or badly injured in the crash. When the paper finally arrived, the article was about George— the explosions and their possible connection with the crash— when it should have been about the march. The march was shaping up to be a kind of ending to a part of my life different from the way it ended the first time when I retreated here to the gas station, unable to do much of anything.

"I wanted to kill George for what he did to spoil it. I talked to him yesterday and told him that he was never again to live where I'm living or talk to anyone who is part of my life. And last night I had a dream that the Feds found out the gas station is a money-laundering operation and they shut it all down, there was nothing left—the mechanics, the house, the job, nothing—and when I woke up, I felt good. I was relieved to see it all go. I still feel free of the prison I've built for myself."

"Now that you're free of George—sort of—the gas station, the mechanics, the boss, and everything else, what are you going to do?"

"I don't know. Maybe I'll get some more car repair training from the mechanics, and then give the boss two weeks' notice and pack up my car and become … I don't know … an 'Itinerant Auto Mechanic.' I'll work for a while as a mechanic at a service station and save up a little money and then rent a barn where I can live and work on large sculptures, and join a group of other artists who I can learn from, and then do some more work to pay the bills, and live like that."

"That sounds very nice, but what about me, what about us?" The two of them laughed, knowing where this was heading.

"I'm glad you asked. What I have in mind is the two of us doing this together. You could be the office manager at the service station where I work, or you could be a waitress or a secretary or anything else you want to be."

Laughing deeply and burrowing her head into Robert's chest, Madeline said, "You read my mind. That's my dream, too."

That night, Robert was unable to sleep as he lay in bed next to Madeline. Early the next morning, after Madeline had left to attend a department meeting, Robert stood in front of the gas station office, enjoying the warmth of the sun on his face. After a while, he walked to the place where the orange juice can lay. On picking it up, he couldn't help checking to see if there was a note inside—which in fact there was. Robert spread out the piece of paper on which was printed: *sorry. james*.

Robert crumpled the paper and stuffed it back into the can before walking back toward the office. About ten feet shy of the large rusted trash barrel next to the gas pump, he tossed the orange juice can in a lazy arc into the drum.

Printed in Great Britain
by Amazon

20330029R00112